STORIES FROM PULPHOUSE:
THE HARDBACK MAGAZINE

Edited by
KRISTINE KATHRYN RUSCH

PUBLISHING

Stories from *Pulphouse: The Hardback Magazine*
Published by WMG Publishing Inc.
Cover and interior design copyright © 2021 WMG Publishing Inc.
Cover art copyright © by stocksnapper/Depositphotos

ISBN-13: 978-1-56146-498-2
ISBN-10: 1-56146-498-8

Introductions © 2021 by Kristine Kathryn Rusch
"While She Was Out" © 2021 by the estate of Edward Bryant. First published
in *Pulphouse: The Hardback Magazine*, edited by Kristine Kathryn Rusch, 1988.
"The Murderer Chooses Sterility" © 2021 by Bradley Denton. First published
in *Pulphouse: The Hardback Magazine*, edited by Kristine Kathryn Rusch, 1990.
"The Two-Headed Man" © 2021 by Nancy A. Collins. First published
in *Pulphouse: The Hardback Magazine*, edited by Kristine Kathryn Rusch, 1990.
"Savage Breasts" © 2021 by Nina Kiriki Hoffman. First published in *Pulphouse:
The Hardback Magazine*, edited by Kristine Kathryn Rusch, 1988.
"Bits and Pieces" © 2021 by Lisa Tuttle. First published in *Pulphouse: The Hardback
Magazine*, edited by Kristine Kathryn Rusch, 1990.
"Willie of the Jungle" © 2021 by Steve Perry. First published in *Pulphouse: The
Hardback Magazine*, edited by Kristine Kathryn Rusch, 1989.
"Clearance to Land" © 2021 by Adam-Troy Castro. First published in *Pulphouse:
The Hardback Magazine*, edited by Kristine Kathryn Rusch, 1989.
"The Soft Whisper of Midnight Snow" © 2021 by Charles de Lint. First published
in *Pulphouse: The Hardback Magazine*, edited by Kristine Kathryn Rusch, 1988.
"Offerings" © 2021 by Susan Palwick. First published in *Pulphouse: The Hardback
Magazine*, edited by Kristine Kathryn Rusch, 1990.
"On a Phantom Tide" © 2021 by William F. Wu. First published in *Pulphouse: The
Hardback Magazine*, edited by Kristine Kathryn Rusch, 1990.

Dedication:
For Dean Wesley Smith and Debra Gray De Noux
—this book is ours, guys.

And especially for Bill Trojan
—we couldn't have done this without you.

Contents

Contents

The New Introduction

Wow. Looking back on something from thirty years ago is *weird*. I have a strong memory of the early days of *Pulphouse*, particularly the Hardback Magazine, but I'd forgotten a lot of things. Some of those things were good things. I'd also remembered too many of the bad things.

I'm not doing a best-of here, because what is best-of right now might not be best-of twenty years from now. I'm proud of what we did with the Hardback. Many of the writers we picked as new writers, often with their first sales, are still around.

Some of the stories we had in the magazine are dated now, but not for the reasons you'd think. You see, we conceived of *Pulphouse* as a "dangerous" magazine, meaning we were publishing stories that the editors of other publications often turned down, not because the stories were bad, but because they dealt with topics that publishers deemed "unsaleable."

Some of those stories are now mainstream. Some use a very 1980s way of describing things that have moved into the culture in a slightly different way. (I'm thinking in particular of stories that featured what we would now call non-binary characters. The language from the time is offensive to readers now, but we didn't have the same language back then.)

With that in mind, some of the stories you'll read here won't seem dangerous at all. They'll seem normal. Because we were often ahead of the trend, buying what became mainstream a decade or two or three later.

And a handful of these stories are *still* dangerous, in the sense that no one else is publishing this kind of work. I'll try to point these things out in the introductions.

One of my criteria for choosing the stories in this volume was this: Could I remember the story *without rereading it* three decades after the story first entranced me? The answer is *yes* for each one of these stories.

Then I reread, decided whether or not the story fit into what I was doing here, and ended up with ten stories out of oh, so many that we published in those twelve volumes.

After thumbing through the volumes, I decided to pull the introduction from *The Best of Pulphouse: The Hardback Magazine*, published by St. Martin's Press in 1991. That introduction, written while *Pulphouse* still existed, explains the origins better than I can from a distance of thirty years.

It also captures some of the breathlessness of the time. When I wrote that, I had no idea what was coming. I would become the first female editor of *The Magazine of Fantasy & Science Fiction*, and while I would continue to edit books for Pulphouse Publishing, my days of editing magazines there ended, and Dean Wesley Smith took over.

There was a freedom in editing stories for a limited edition volume with a set readership. I could publish stories that offended, stories that experimented, and stories that surprised. I could publish stories about LGBTQ people and people of color without getting hate mail. (The early 1990s were a different and difficult time.) I could publish stories with strong women and stories with images that still raise my eyebrows even today.

I brought a lot of those attitudes to *F&SF* when I edited there, but with that came the hate mail and the not-so-subtle worries of the publisher that some of the "outlier" stories (as he called it) would damage his magazine.

It was his magazine. I sometimes lost those fights. I never lost the fights at *Pulphouse* because I was the co-owner of the publishing company. In the F&SF years, I learned a lot about editorial courage, the economics of a large subscriber base, and the tyranny of the almighty dollar.

Some of the stories in this volume still would not show up in the mainstream publications of today, although more of them would. (Thank heavens.) The world has changed dramatically since *The Hardback Magazine* existed.

Sometimes editing it feels like yesterday; sometimes I find it unreal that the entire project even existed, born as it was on the scarred dining room table in my truly crummy one-bedroom apartment.

Sometimes I think courage is simply ignorance of the rules. Or maybe a much-too-healthy ego. To this day, I don't understand why stories about people who are not white and middle class didn't get through the gatekeepers in publishing for decades.

I'm proud of what we did with *The Hardback Magazine*. We launched careers, changed some minds, and made a difference.

That doesn't happen very often, in any career.

—Kristine Kathryn Rusch
Las Vegas, Nevada
April 3, 2021

The Original Introduction

I can never pinpoint the exact moment when the craziness started. Perhaps it began the first time Dean Wesley Smith and I gazed at each other (across a crowded kitchen in New Mexico— add violins or an ominous orchestral rumble, depending on your point of view.) Perhaps it started during those late night conversations in his apartment in Eugene, conversations that began with "Why doesn't somebody...?" and ended with "Yeah! What a great idea!" Sometimes I think that we both were individually crazy (I did, after all, work for seven years at a very political, listener-sponsored radio station for relaxation—and Dean, well, Dean gave away *free* 52 issues of a magazine he wrote, edited, designed and published) and when we got together, the insanity reached critical mass.

No matter. The spark of Pulphouse Publishing might be lost in the sands of time, but the memories remain. We started *Pulphouse: The Hardback Magazine* for a variety of reasons. Dean's first novel, *Laying the Music to Rest*, had just been rejected by a major publisher because it couldn't decide how to market the book.[1] A number of my stories had been returned by my regular editors because the stories were "too weird." We complained that there weren't enough markets—especially markets open to unusual work—and we decided to do something about it.

Of course, we had no idea what we were getting into.

We did have some experience. I knew, from my radio days, that in order to be experimental, we could not be tied to a subscription or advertising base. Too many subscribers revoke their subscriptions because of dirty words or sex scenes. (Just that year, an editor had warned me that even though he was publishing one of my stories, he was worried that he would lose a lot of subscribers because of a scene in which a woman raped a man.) Too many advertisers tried to control content they viewed as potentially harmful to their product or their image. I had also spent my years at the station editing a nightly newscast. I understood that content had to flow together and that deadlines were firm.

Dean, on the other hand, published a writer's magazine for a number of years. He knew that there was more to a magazine than its editorial content. Design, marketing, and a unified vision were important. His years as an architect gave him both design skills and an understanding of the importance of details. His law and business experience helped with the publishing side.

We studied the market and decided that, with our skills, we could put together a hardback book filled with short stories by name and unknown writers and sell it to the collector's market. The collecting field was going through a boom during that period, and would go for anything unusual and different; a hardback magazine with the freedom to publish stories in any (and every) genre seemed to us to be unusual—and worthwhile. We didn't expect to sell a lot of copies, but we set our price structure so that we didn't have to. We called the book a magazine instead of an anthology because it was quarterly, available by *subscription*. Originally it was going to have interior advertising and more columns. (Look inside Issue One. Our one and only ad appears there, and shows why we decided against advertising.)

Dean spent hours and hours, sometimes going days without sleep, designing the look of the magazine. He also read slush. I read manuscripts too, and contacted writers. Jack Williamson agreed to let us reprint his essays on writing. Steve Rasnic Tem and William F. Wu sent us wonderful stories. Kij Johnson was the first new name to rise above the slush pile. We grew excited with our growing project.

Then we tried to contact other writers, and discovered that we couldn't explain what a "hardback magazine" was. Dean had already decided to do a mock-up of the magazine. Detail-oriented perfectionist that he is, he wanted everything to be exactly right in the first issue. That meant we needed to have a practice step in between.

A Pulphouse tradition, Issue Zero, was born. Issue Zero (which we have done on all of our projects since) is a mock-up, done to show exactly what the project will look like, and to work out the bugs in the system. Issue Zero of the Hardback Magazine shows that we expected the magazine to be smaller in size and scope than it turned out to be. It also proved to be the smartest thing we did.

Dean used Issue Zero to attract bookstores. I sent copies of it to my favorite writers. Many responded with stories. We gathered an impressive line-up: Kate Wilhelm, Charles de Lint, Edward Bryant. Then I got my phone call from Harlan Ellison.

Actually, it wasn't a phone call. He left a message on my answering machine. "I received your Pulphouse loss leader," he said. "I want to talk to you about it." He left his phone number and hung up.

I called him back before I had time to worry about what he wanted. (After all, the back of my brain reasoned, we did call *Pulphouse* a "Dangerous Magazine." Was he objecting? Were we too close to *Dangerous Visions?*) When Harlan came on the line, my worries evaporated. He was effusive. He thought we were brilliant, absolutely brilliant, to do a mock-up of our product, and for that reason alone, decided to contribute a story to our effort.

He later explained to me what we had done right. Not only had we some impressive names already in our roster (including people who rarely wrote for anthologies), but we proved that we could produce a product. So many magazines appear as announcements in writers' publications and as invitations to writers, but somehow disappear around payment and production time, that writers and agents naturally mistrust any new publication. Most would-be magazine publishers never realize the costs involved. We, at least, were thinking about production as well as editorial content.

As the list of contributors for the first issue began to grow, so did book dealers' interest. People we had never met ordered the product in quantities we hadn't even dreamed of. Within a month, we doubled our projected sales, and sold out our first issue before it appeared in August. And we realized we were in over our heads.

Dean and I are writers, creative types who pride ourselves on our lack of organization and messy desks. (Dean, striving for perfection even in clutter, tends to have a *perfectly* messy desk.) We knew nothing about shipping, packing, or filing. We had enough work for the two of us, plus two more without trying to stay organized. If we had to be organized, we would be overloaded.

But to run a business of the size that Pulphouse had become in just a few short months, we needed to be organized or we would fail.

Enter Debra Gray Cook. Debb was a friend of Dean's who worked as a secretary/receptionist for a poster company. She took a half-time job at a video store because she was bored. She had been offering her assistance for months. We finally took her up on it.

Bringing in Debb was the second most intelligent thing we did.

Debb immediately organized us. Her job at the poster company had taught her about shipping. She spent a hot, dismal weekend with us (volunteering her labor—and we worked all night and into the next day) in Dean's unairconditioned second floor apartment shipping out Pulphouse's first issue. By the end of the marathon shipping session, we were covered with sweat and Styrofoam. Debb and I had rug burns from kneeling on the rough carpet, and shoving books into boxes. Dean had thrown out his back from carrying books up and down two flights of stairs (never do shipping from the second floor), Debb could barely move her arms from pulling the tape gun. We were too tired to celebrate.

But celebrate we eventually did. And we were well into Issue 2 by the time we saw that the reviews from the first issue were positive. (Boy, was I relieved.) Pulphouse Publishing grew into an entity all its own. First Dean quit his day job. I followed, and Debb followed not long after that. We acquired Axolotl Press, started *Author's Choice Monthly*, and found an office. We hired help, most notably Mark Budz, who is now the editor of our Short Story Paperback Line. The office grew another story. At this writing, we have 14 employees, and more projects than I care to think about. Every time we announce something new, people tell us that we're crazy, that what we're trying is impossible. And we love proving them wrong.

But we never could have done this without the help and advice of Bill Trojan (skeptic book dealer with a heart of gold), Nina Kiriki Hoffman (typesetter/proofer/good friend *extraordinaire*), Phil Barnhart (former boss—a man who knows potential when he sees it[thank god]), Alan Bard Newcomer (computer/technical wizard), and Lynn Adams (whose creative touches have added more to the Pulphouse memorabilia line than anyone else's). These folks have been with us from the beginning. The other folks, whose contributions have been almost as significant, are listed on the acknowledgments page. These people have given more than we could ever hope for.

We have a wonderful group of friends. They've supported us well.

As has the science fiction community. Issue 12, the last issue of the hardback, appeared this summer, and a number of people are sad to see it go. So are we. But the hardback served its time. We're moving on to larger, crazier projects with the potential for a larger audience. Dean Wesley Smith is now editing our flagship: *Pulphouse: A Weekly Magazine*. By the time you read this, he will already have more than 12 issues completed and shipped (in our air-conditioned shipping office on the first floor, thank you.) It took the hardback three years to get that far. I hope that the Weekly will have as much success and acclaim. It already does, from my point of view.

I am pleased, though, that Gordon Van Gelder helped us do this book. Only 1250 copies of each issue of the hardback magazine exist. Although a number of stories were reprinted in year's best anthologies, a number weren't. I wish we could find a paperback publisher for the entire run (even though I know I am dreaming). But for every story included in this volume, there are five that I would have liked to have added. For every author, there are a dozen more I would have liked to include. Picking the stories for this volume was one of the most difficult tasks I've ever done.

So, if you get a chance, search out copies of the hardback magazine. Look up stories by newer writers, like Marina Fitch, Ken Wisman, and Kij Johnson. Keep your eyes open for stories of theirs; they'll be showing up in lots of publications. We weren't able to include stories by Damon Knight, Robert Sheckley, or Kate Wilhelm either. Please remember that what you have in your hand is just a sampling of what we have done in the hardback—and of what Pulphouse Publishing plans to do in the future. And above all, enjoy.

—Kristine Kathryn Rusch
Eugene, Oregon

1. The editor who did publish the book, Brian Thomsen, didn't have that problem. He published the book as science fiction. It wound up as a finalist for the Bram Stoker Award for the best first horror novel of the year. Evidently, there were people who liked it regardless of whatever label it wore.

While She Was Out

EDWARD BRYANT

Introduction

I started Volume One with this story, started the St. Martins' Best of Pulphouse with it, and need to start with it here.

The story is tough and suspenseful. It was quite a shocker back in the day, because of what is now a pretty unsurprising twist. Strong women were just coming to their own in fiction in 1991 (yes, I know. Weird). I like to think we helped start that trend, but we didn't. We were on the leading edge of it, along with some really great mystery writers, like Sara Paretsky and Sue Grafton.

Edward W. Bryant, Jr. was a great supporter of Pulphouse. He was on the cutting edge of short fiction in the 1970s, but like so many writers, ended up writing less and less and reviewing more and more. Ed was well known in science fiction circles, but not as well known as he should have been as a writer.

"While She Was Out" appeared as Ed started to slow down as a writer. He published less and less throughout the 1990s, and even though he passed away in 2017, he published no original material (that I can find) during the last two decades of his life.

What a loss to readers. At least we still have the stories he did write, like this one, which is one of my all-time favorites.

While She Was Out

Edward Bryant

It was what her husband said then that was the last straw.

"Christ," muttered Kenneth disgustedly from the family room.

He grasped a Bud longneck in one red-knuckled hand, the cable remote tight in the other. This was the time of night when he generally fell into the largest number of stereotypes. "I swear to God you're on the rag three weeks out of every month. PMS, my ass."

Della Myers deliberately bit down on what she wanted to answer. P*X*MS, she thought. That's what the twins' teacher had called it last week over coffee after the parent-teacher conference Kenneth had skipped. Pre-holiday syndrome. It took a genuine effort not to pick up the cordless Northwestern Bell phone and brain Kenneth with one savage, cathartic swipe. "I'm going out."

"So?" said her husband. "This is Thursday. Can't be the auto mechanics made simple for wusses. Self defense?" He shook his head. "That's every other Tuesday. Something new, honey? Maybe a therapy group?"

"I'm going to Southeast Plaza. I need to pick up some things."

5

"Get the extra-absorbent ones," said her husband. He grinned and thumbed up the volume. ESPN was bringing in wide shots of something that looked vaguely like group tennis from some sweatylooking third-world country.

"Wrapping paper," she said. "I'm getting some gift-wrap and ribbon." Were there fourth-world countries? she wondered. Would they accept political refugees from America? "Will you put the twins to bed by nine?"

"Stallone's on HBO at nine," Kenneth said. "I'll bag 'em out by half-past eight."

"Fine." She didn't argue.

"I'll give them a good bedtime story." He paused. "The Princess and the Pea."

"Fine." Della shrugged on her long down-filled coat. Any more, she did her best not to swallow the bait. "I told them they could each have a chocolate chip cookie with their milk."

"Christ, Della. Why the hell don't we just adopt the dentist? Maybe give him an automatic monthly debit from the checking account?"

"One cookie apiece," she said, implacable.

Kenneth shrugged, apparently resigned.

She picked up the keys to the Subaru. "I won't be long."

"Just be back by breakfast."

Della stared at him. What if I don't come back at all? She had actually said that once. Kenneth had smiled and asked whether she was going to run away with the gypsies, or maybe go off to join some pirates. It had been a temptation to say yes, dammit, yes, I'm going. But there were the twins. Della suspected pirates didn't take along their children. "Don't worry," she said. I've got nowhere else to go. But she didn't say that aloud.

Della turned and went upstairs to the twins' room to tell them good night. Naturally they both wanted to go with her to the mall. Each was afraid she wasn't going to get the hottest item in the Christmas doll department—the Little BeeDee Birth

Defect Baby. There had been a run on the BeeDee, but Della had shopped for the twins early. "Daddy's going to tell you a story," she promised. The pair wasn't impressed.

"I want to see Santa," Terri said, with dogged, five-year-old insistence.

"You both saw Santa. Remember?"

"I forgot some things. An' I want to tell him again about BeeDee."

"Me, too," said Tammi. With Tammi, it was always "me too."

"Maybe this weekend," said Della.

"Will Daddy remember our cookies?" said Terri.

Before she exited the front door, Della took the chocolate chip cookies from the kitchen closet and set the sack on the stairstep where Kenneth could not fail to stumble over it.

"So long," she called.

"Bring me back something great from the mall," he said. His only other response was to heighten the crowd noise from Upper Zambosomewhere-or-other.

Sleety snow was falling, the accumulation beginning to freeze on the streets. Della was glad she had the Subaru. So far this winter, she hadn't needed to use the four-wheel drive, but tonight the reality of having it reassured her.

Southeast Plaza was a mess. This close to Christmas, the normally spacious parking lots were jammed. Della took a chance and circled the row of spaces nearest to the mall entrances. If she were lucky, she'd be able to react instantly to someone's backup lights and snaffle a parking place within five seconds of its being vacated. That didn't happen. She cruised the second row, the third. Then—There! She reacted without thinking, seeing the vacant spot just beyond a metallic blue van. She swung the Subaru to the left.

And stamped down hard on the brake.

Some moron had parked an enormous barge of an ancient Plymouth so that it overlapped two diagonal spaces.

The Subaru slid to a stop with its nose about half an inch from the Plymouth's dinosaurian bumper. In the midst of her shock and sudden anger, Della saw the chrome was pocked with rust. The Subaru's headlights reflected back at her.

She said something unpleasant, the kind of language she usually only thought in dark silence. Then she backed her car out of the truncated space and resumed the search for parking. What Della eventually found was a free space on the extreme perimeter of the lot. She resigned herself to trudging a quarter mile through the slush. She hadn't worn boots. The icy water crept into her flats, soaked her toes.

"Shit," she said. "Shit shit shit."

Her shortest-distance-between-two-points course took her past the Plymouth hogging the two parking spots. Della stopped a moment, contemplating the darkened behemoth. It was a dirty gold with the remnants of a vinyl roof peeling away like the flaking of a scabrous scalp. In the glare of the mercury vapor lamp, she could see that the rocker panels were riddled with rust holes. Odd. So much corrosion didn't happen in the dry Colorado air. She glanced curiously at the rear license plate. It was obscured with dirty snow.

She stared at the huge old car and realized she was getting angry. Not just irritated. Real, honest-to-god, hardcore pissed off. What kind of imbeciles would take up two parking spaces on a rotten night just two weeks before Christmas?

Ones that drove a vintage, not-terribly-kept-up Plymouth, obviously.

Without even thinking about what she was doing, Della took out the spiral notebook from her handbag. She flipped to the blank page past tomorrow's grocery list and uncapped the fine-tip marker (it was supposed to write across anything—in this snow, it had *better*) and scrawled a message:

· · · ·

DEAR JERK, IT'S GREAT YOU COULD USE UP TWO PARKING SPACES ON A NIGHT LIKE THIS. EVER HEAR OF THE JOY OF SHARING?

She paused, considering; then appended:

—A CONCERNED FRIEND

Della folded the paper as many times as she could, to protect it from the wet, then slipped it under the driver's-side wiper blade.

It wouldn't do any good—she was sure this was the sort of driver who ordinarily would have parked illegally in the handicapped zone—but it made her feel better. Della walked on to the mall entrance and realized she was smiling.

She bought some rolls of foil wrapping paper for the adult gifts —assuming she actually gave Kenneth anything she'd bought for him—and an ample supply of Strawberry Shortcake pattern for the twins' presents. Della decided to splurge—she realized she was getting tired—and selected a package of pre-tied ribbon bows rather than simply taking a roll. She also bought a package of tampons.

Della wandered the mall for a little while, checking out the shoe stores, looking for something on sale in deep blue, a pair she could wear after Kenneth's office party for staff and spouses. What she *really* wanted were some new boots. Time enough for those after the holiday when the prices went down. Nothing appealed to her. Della knew she should be shopping for Kenneth's family in Nebraska. She couldn't wait forever to mail off their packages.

The hell with it. Della realized she was simply delaying

returning home. Maybe she *did* need a therapy group, she thought. There was no relish to the thought of spending another night sleeping beside Kenneth, listening to the snoring that was interrupted only by the grinding of teeth. She thought that the sound of Kenneth's jaws moving against one another must be like hearing a speeded-up recording of continental drift.

She looked at her watch. A little after nine. No use waiting any longer. She did up the front of her coat and joined the flow of shoppers out into the snow.

Della realized, as she passed the rusted old Plymouth, that something wasn't the same. *What's wrong with this picture?* It was the note. It wasn't there. Probably it had slipped out from under the wiper blade with the wind and the water. Maybe the flimsy notebook paper had simply dissolved.

She no longer felt like writing another note. She dismissed the irritating lumber barge from her reality and walked on to her car.

Della let the Subaru warm up for thirty seconds (the consumer auto mechanics class had told her not to let the engine idle for the long minutes she had once believed necessary) and then slipped the shift into reverse.

The passenger compartment flooded with light.

She glanced into the rearview mirror and looked quickly away. A bright, glaring eye had stared back. Another quivered in the side mirror.

"Jesus Christ," she said under her breath. "The crazies are out tonight." She hit the clutch with one foot, the brake with the other, and waited for the car behind her to remove itself. Nothing happened. The headlights in the mirror flicked to bright. "Dammit." Della left the Subaru in neutral and got out of the car.

She shaded her eyes and squinted. The front of the car behind hers looked familiar. It was the gold Plymouth.

Two unseen car-doors clicked open and chunked shut again.

The lights abruptly went out and Della blinked, her eyes trying to adjust to the dim mercury vapor illumination from the pole a few car-lengths away.

She felt a cold thrill of unease in her belly and turned back toward the car.

"I've got a gun," said a voice. "Really." It sounded male and young. "I'll aim at your snatch first."

Someone else giggled, high and shrill.

Della froze in place. This couldn't be happening. It absolutely could not.

Her eyes were adjusting, the glare-phantoms drifting out to the limit of her peripheral vision and vanishing. She saw three figures in front of her, then a fourth. She didn't see a gun.

"Just what do you think you're doing?" she said.

"Not doing *nothin'*, yet." That, she saw, was the black one. He stood to the left of the white kid who had claimed to have a gun. The pair was bracketed by a boy who looked Chinese or Vietnamese and a young man with dark, Hispanic good looks. All four looked to be in their late teens or very early twenties. Four young men. Four ethnic groups represented. Della repressed a giggle she thought might be the first step toward hysteria.

"So what are you guys? Working on your merit badge in tolerance? Maybe selling magazine subscriptions?" Della immediately regretted saying that. Her husband was always riding her for smarting off.

"Funny lady," said the Hispanic. "We just happen to get along." He glanced to his left. "You laughing, Huey?"

The black shook his head. "Too cold. I'm shiverin' out here. I didn't bring no clothes for this."

"Easy way to fix that, man," said the white boy. To Della, he said, "Vinh, Tomas, Huey, me, we all got similar interests, you know?"

"Listen—" Della started to say.

"Chuckie," said the black Della now assumed was Huey, "Let's us just shag out of here, okay?"

"*Chuckie?*" said Della.

"Shut up!" said Chuckie. To Huey, he said, "Look, we came up here for a vacation, right? The word is fun." He said to Della, "Listen, we were having a good time until we saw you stick the note under the wiper." His eyes glistened in the vapor-lamp glow. "I don't like getting any static from some 'burb-bitch just 'cause she's on the rag."

"For God's sake," said Della disgustedly. She decided he didn't really have a gun. "Screw off!" The exhaust vapor from the Subaru spiraled up around her. "I'm leaving, boys."

"Any trouble here, Miss?" said a new voice. Everyone looked. It was one of the mall rent-a-cops, bulky in his fur trimmed jacket and Russian-styled cap. His hand lay casually across the unsnapped holster flap at his hip.

"Not if these underage creeps move their barge so I can back out," said Della.

"How about it, guys?" said the rent-a-cop.

Now there *was* a gun, a dark pistol, in Chuckie's hand, and he pointed it at the rent-a-cop's face. "Naw," Chuckie said. "This was gonna be a vacation, but what the heck. No witnesses, I reckon."

"For God's sake," said the rent-a-cop, starting to back away.

Chuckie grinned and glanced aside at his friends. "Remember the security guy at the mall in Tucson?" To Della, he said, "Most of these rent-a-pig companies don't give their guys any ammo. Liability laws and all that shit. Too bad." He lifted the gun purposefully.

. The rent-a-cop went for his pistol anyway. Chuckie shot him in the face. Red pulp sprayed out the back of his skull and stained the slush as the man's body flopped back and forth, spasming.

"For chrissake," said Chuckie in exasperation. "Enough already. Relax, man." He leaned over his victim and deliberately aimed and fired, aimed and fired. The second shot entered the rent-a-cop's left eye. The third shattered his teeth.

Della's eyes recorded everything as though she were a movie camera. Everything was moving in slow motion and she was numb. She tried to make things speed up. Without thinking about the decision, she spun and made for her car door. She knew it was hopeless.

"Chuckie!"

"So? Where's she gonna go? We got her blocked. I'll just put one through her windshield and we can go out and pick up a couple of sixpacks, maybe hit the late show at some other mall."

Della heard him fire one more time. Nothing tore through the back of her skull. He was still blowing apart the rent-a-cop's head.

She slammed into the Subaru's driver seat and punched the doorlock switch, for all the good that would do. Della hit the four-wheeldrive switch. *That* was what Chuckie hadn't thought about. She jammed the gearshift into first, gunned the engine, and popped the clutch. The Subaru barely protested as the front tires clawed and bounced over the six-inch concrete row barrier. The barrier screeched along the underside of the frame. Then the rear wheels were over and the Subaru fishtailed momentarily.

Don't over-correct, she thought. It was a prayer.

The Subaru straightened out and Della was accelerating down the mall's outer perimeter service road, slush spraying to either side. Now what? she thought. People must have heard the shots. The lot would be crawling with cops.

But in the meantime—

The lights, bright and blinding, blasted against her mirrors.

Della stamped the accelerator to the floor.

This was crazy! This didn't happen to people—not to *real* people. The mall security man's blood in the snow had been real enough.

In the rearview, there was a sudden flash just above the left-side headlight, then another. It was a muzzle-blast, Della realized. They were shooting at her. It was just like on TV. The scalp on the back of her head itched. Would she feel it when the bullet crashed through?

The twins! Kenneth. She wanted to see them all, to be safely with them. Just be anywhere but here!

Della spun the wheel, ignoring the stop sign and realizing that the access road dead-ended. She could go right or left, so went right. She thought it was the direction of home. Not a good choice. The lights were all behind her now; she could see nothing but darkness ahead. Della tried to remember what lay beyond the mall on this side. There were housing developments, both completed and under construction.

There had to be a 7-Eleven, a filling station, *something*. Anything. But there wasn't, and then the pavement ended. At first the road was suddenly rougher, the potholes yawning deeper. Then the slushmarked asphalt stopped. The Subaru bounced across the gravel; within thirty yards, the gravel deteriorated to roughly graded dirt. The dirt surface more properly could be called mud.

A wooden barrier loomed ahead, the reflective stripes and lightly falling snow glittering in the headlights.

It *was* like on TV, Della thought. She gunned the engine and ducked sideways, even with the dash, as the Subaru plowed into the barrier. She heard a sickening *crack* and shattered windshield glass sprayed down around her. Della felt the car veer. She tried to sit upright again, but the auto was spinning too fast.

The Subaru swung a final time and smacked firm against a low grove of young pine. The engine coughed and stalled. Della hit the light switch. She smelled the overwhelming tang of crushed pine needles flooding with the snow through the space where the windshield had been. The engine groaned when she twisted the key, didn't start.

Della risked a quick look around. The Plymouth's lights were visible, but the car was farther back than she had dared hope. The size of the lights wasn't increasing and the beams pointed up at a steep angle. Probably the heavy Plymouth had slid in the slush, gone off the road, was stuck for good.

She tried the key, and again the engine didn't catch. She heard something else—voices getting closer. Della took the key out of the ignition and glanced around the dark passenger compartment. Was there anything she could use? Anything at all? Not in the glovebox. She knew there was nothing there but the owner's manual and a large pack of sugarless spearmint gum.

The voices neared.

Della reached under the dash and tugged the trunk release. Then she rolled down the window and slipped out into the darkness. She wasn't too stunned to forget that the overhead-light would go on if she opened the door.

At least one of the boys had a flashlight. The beam flickered and danced along the snow.

Della stumbled to the rear of the Subaru. By feel, she found the toolbox. With her other hand, she sought out the lug wrench. Then she moved away from the car.

She wished she had a gun. She wished she had learned to *use* a gun. That had been something tagged for a vague future when she'd finished her consumer mechanics course and the self defense workshop, and had some time again to take another night course. It wasn't, she had reminded herself, that she was paranoid. Della simply wanted to be better prepared for the exigencies of living in the city. The suburbs weren't *the city* to Kenneth, but if you were a girl from rural Montana, they were.

She hadn't expected this.

She hunched down. Her nose told her the shelter she had found was a hefty clump of sagebrush. She was perhaps twenty yards from the Subaru now. The boys were making no attempt at stealth. She heard them talking to each other as the flashlight beam bobbed around her stalled car.

"So, she in there chilled with her brains all over the wheel?" said Tomas, the Hispanic kid.

"You an optimist?" said Chuckie. He laughed, a high-pitched giggle. "No, she ain't here, you dumb shit. This one's a tough lady." Then he said, "Hey, lookie there!"

"What you doin'?" said Huey. "We ain't got time for that."

"Don't be too sure. Maybe we can use this."

What had he found? Della wondered.

"Now we do what?" said Vinh. He had a slight accent.

"This be the West," said Huey. "I guess now we're mountain men, just like in the movies."

"Right," said Chuckie. "Track her. There's mud. There's snow. How far can she get?"

"There's the trail," said Tomas. "Shine the light over there. She must be pretty close."

Della turned. Hugging the toolbox, trying not to let it clink or clatter, she fled into the night.

They cornered her a few minutes later.

Or it could have been an hour. There was no way she could read her watch. All Della knew was that she had run; she had run and she had attempted circling around to where she might have a shot at making it to the distant lights of the shopping mall. Along the way, she'd felt the brush clawing at her denim jeans and the mud and slush attempting to suck down her shoes. She tried to make out shapes in the cloudedover dark, evaluating every murky form as a potential hiding place.

"Hey, baby," said Huey from right in front of her.

Della recoiled, feinted to the side, collided painfully with a wooden fence. The boards gave only slightly. She felt a long splinter drive through the down coat and spear into her shoulder. When Della jerked away, she felt the splinter tear away from its board and then break off.

The flashlight snapped on, the beam at first blinding her,

then lowering to focus on her upper body. From their voices, she knew all four were there. Della wanted to free a hand to pull the splinter loose from her shoulder. Instead she continued cradling the blue plastic toolbox.

"Hey," said Chuckie, "what's in that thing? Family treasure, maybe?"

Della remained mute. She'd already gotten into trouble enough, wising off.

"Let's see," said Chuckie. "Show us, Della-honey."

She stared at his invisible face.

Chuckie giggled. "Your driver's license, babe. In your purse. In the car."

Shit, she thought.

"Lousy picture." Chuckie. "I think maybe we're gonna make your face match it." Again, that ghastly laugh. "Meantime, let's see what's in the box, okay?"

"Jewels, you think?" said Vinh.

"Naw, I don't think," said his leader. "But maybe she was makin' the bank deposit or something." He addressed Della, "You got enough goodies for us, maybe we can be bought off."

No chance, she thought. They want everything. My money, my rings, my watch. She tried to swallow, but her throat was too dry. My life.

"Open the box," said Chuckie, voice mean now.

"Open the box," said Tomas. Huey echoed him. The four started chanting, "Open the box, open the box, open the box."

"All right," she almost screamed. "I'll do it." They stopped their chorus. Someone snickered. Her hands moving slowly, Della's brain raced. Do it, she thought. But be careful. So careful. She let the lug wrench rest across her palm below the toolbox. With her other hand, she unsnapped the catch and slid up the lid toward the four. She didn't think any of them could see in, though the flashlight beam was focused now on the toolbox lid.

Della reached inside, as deliberately as she could, trying to betray nothing of what she hoped to do. It all depended upon what lay on top. Her bare fingertips touched the cold steel of the crescent wrench. Her fingers curled around the handle.

"This is pretty dull," said Tomas. "Let's just rape her."

Now!

She withdrew the wrench, cocked her wrist back and hurled the tool about two feet above the flashlight's glare. Della snapped it just like her daddy had taught her to throw a hardball. She hadn't liked baseball all that much. But now—

The wrench crunched something and Chuckie screamed. The flashlight dropped to the snow.

Snapping shut the toolbox, Della sprinted between Chuckie and the one she guessed was Huey.

The black kid lunged for her and slipped in the muck, toppling face-first into the slush. Della had a peripheral glimpse of Tomas leaping toward her, but his leading foot came down on the back of Huey's head, grinding the boy's face into the mud. Huey's scream bubbled; Tomas cursed and tumbled forward, trying to stop himself with out-thrust arms.

All Della could think as she gained the darkness was, I should have grabbed the light.

She heard the one she thought was Vinh, laughing. "Cripes, guys, neat. Just like Moe and Curley and that other one."

"Shut up," said Chuckie's voice. It sounded pinched and in pain. "Shut the fuck up." The timbre squeaked and broke. "Get up, you dorks. Get the bitch."

Sticks and stones—Della thought. Was she getting hysterical?

There was no good reason not to.

As she ran—and stumbled—across the nightscape, Della could feel the long splinter moving with the movement of the muscles in her shoulder. The feeling of it, not just the pain, but the sheer, physical sensation of intrusion, nauseated her.

I've got to stop, she thought. I've got to rest. I've got to think.

Della stumbled down the side of a shallow gulch and found she was splashing across a shallow, frigid stream. Water. It triggered something. Disregarding the cold soaking her flats and numbing her feet, she turned and started upstream, attempting to splash as a little as possible. This had worked, she seemed to recall, in Uncle Tom's Cabin, as well as a lot of bad prison escape movies.

The boys were hardly experienced mountain men. They weren't Indian trackers. This ought to take care of her trail.

After what she estimated to be at least a hundred yards, when her feet felt like blocks of wood and she felt she was losing her balance, Della clambered out of the stream and struggled up the side of the gulch. She found herself in groves of pine, much like the trees where her Subaru had ended its skid. At least the pungent evergreens supplied some shelter against the prairie wind that had started to rise.

She heard noise from down in the gulch. It was music. It made her think of the twins.

"What the fuck are you doing?" Chuckie's voice.

"It's a tribute, man. A gesture." Vinh. "It's his blaster."

Della recognized the tape. Rap music. Run DMC, the Beastie Boys, one of those groups.

"Christ, I didn't mean it." Tomas. "It's her fault."

"Well, he's dead," said Chuckie," and that's it for him. Now turn that shit off. Somebody might hear."

"Who's going to hear?" said Vinh. "Nobody can hear out here. Just us, and her."

"That's the point. She can."

"So what?" said Tomas. "We got the gun, we got the light. She's got nothin' but that stupid box."

"We *had* Huey," said Chuckie. "Now we don't. Shut off the blaster, dammit."

"Okay." Vinh's voice sounded sullen. There was a loud click and the rap echo died.

Della huddled against the rough bark of a pine trunk, hugging the box and herself. The boy's dead, she thought. So? said her common sense. He would have killed you, maybe raped you, tortured you before pulling the trigger. The rest are going to have to die too.

No.

Yes, said her practical side. You have no choice. They started this.

I put the note under the wiper blade.

Get serious. That was harmless. These three are going to kill you.

They will hurt you first, then they'll put the gun inside your mouth and—

Della wanted to cry, to scream. She knew she could not. It was absolutely necessary that she not break now.

Terri, she thought, Tammi. I love you. After a while, she remembered Kenneth. Even you. I love you too. Not much, but some.

"Let's look up above," came the voice from the gully. Chuckie. Della heard the wet scrabbling sounds as the trio scratched and pulled their way up from the stream-bed. As it caught the falling snow, the flashlight looked like the beam from a searchlight at a movie premiere.

Della edged back behind the pine and slowly moved to where the trees were closer together. Boughs laced together, screening her.

"Now what?" said Tomas.

"We split up." Chuckie gestured; the flashlight beam swung wide. "You go through the middle. Vinh and me'll take the sides."

"Then why don't you give me the light?" said Tomas.

"I stole the sucker. It's mine."

"Shit, I could just walk past her."

Chuckie laughed. "Get real, dude. You'll smell her, hear her, somethin'. Trust me."

Tomas said something Della couldn't make out, but the tone was unconvinced.

"Now *do* it," said Chuckie. The light moved off to Della's left. She heard the squelching of wet shoes moving toward her. Evidently Tomas had done some wading in the gully. Either that or the slush was taking its toll.

Tomas couldn't have done better with radar. He came straight for her.

Della guessed the boy was ten feet away from her, five feet, just the other side of the pine. The lug wrench was the spider type, in the shape of a cross. She clutched the black steel of the longest arm and brought her hand back. When she detected movement around the edge of the trunk, she swung with hysterical strength, aiming at his head. Tomas staggered back. The sharp arm of the lug wrench had caught him under the nose, driving the cartilage back up into his face. About a third of the steel was hidden in flesh. "Unh!" He tried to cry out, but all he could utter was, "Unh, unh!"

"Tomas?" Chuckie was yelling. "What the hell are you doing?"

The flashlight flickered across the grove. Della caught a momentary glimpse of Tomas lurching backward with the lug wrench impaled in his face as though he were wearing some hideous Halloween accessory.

"Unh!" said Tomas once more. He backed into a tree, then slid down the trunk until he was seated in the snow. The flashlight beam jerked across that part of the grove again and Della saw Tomas' eyes stare wide open, dark and blank. Blood was running off the ends of the perpendicular lug wrench arms.

"I see her!" someone yelled. "I think she got Tomas. She's a devil!" Vinh.

"So chill her!"

Della heard branches and brush crashing off to her side. She jerked open the plastic toolbox, but her fingers were frozen and the container crashed to the ground. She tried to catch the contents as they cascaded into the slush and the darkness. Her fingers closed on something, one thing.

The handle felt good. It was the wooden-hafted screwdriver, the sharp one with the slot head. Her auto mechanics teacher had approved. Insulated handle, he'd said. Good forged steel shaft. You could use this hummer to pry a tire off its rim.

She didn't even have time to lift it as Vinh crashed into her. His arms and legs wound around her like eels.

"Got her!" he screamed. "Chuckie, come here and shoot her."

They rolled in the viscid, muddy slush. Della worked an arm free. Her good arm. The one with the screwdriver.

There was no question of asking him nicely to let go, of giving warning, of simply aiming to disable. Her self defense teacher had drilled into all the students the basic dictum of do what you can, do what you have to do. No rules, no apologies.

With all her strength, Della drove the screwdriver up into the base of his skull. She thrust and twisted the tool until she felt her knuckles dig into his stiff hair. Vinh screamed, a high keening wail that cracked and shattered as blood spurted out of his nose and mouth, splattering against Della's neck. The Vietnamese boy's arms and legs tensed and then let go as his body vibrated spastically in some sort of fit.

Della pushed him away from her and staggered to her feet. Her nose was full of the odor she remembered from the twins' diaper pail.

She knew she should retrieve the screwdriver, grasp the handle tightly and twist it loose from Vinh's head. She couldn't. All she could do at this point was simply turn and run. Run again. And hope the survivor of the four boys didn't catch her.

But Chuckie had the light, and Chuckie had the gun. She had a feeling Chuckie was in no mood to give up. Chuckie would find her. He would make her pay for the loss of his friends.

But if she had to pay, Della thought, the price would be dear.

Prices, she soon discovered, were subject to change without warning.

With only one remaining pursuer, Della thought she ought to be able to get away. Maybe not easily, but now there was no crossfire of spying eyes, no ganging-up of assailants. There was just one boy left, even if he was a psychopath carrying a loaded pistol.

Della was shaking. It was fatigue, she realized. The endless epinephrine rush of flight and fight. Probably, too, the letdown from just having killed two other human beings. She didn't want to have to think about the momentary sight of blood flowing off the shining ends of the lug wrench, the sensation of how it *felt* when the slotheaded screwdriver drove up into Vinh's brain. But she couldn't order herself to forget these things. It was akin to someone telling her not, under any circumstances, to think about milking a purple cow.

Della tried. No, she thought. Don't think about it at all. She thought about dismembering the purple cow with a chainsaw. Then she heard Chuckie's voice. The boy was still distant, obviously casting around virtually at random in the pine groves. Della stiffened.

"They're cute, Della-honey. I'll give 'em that." He giggled. "Terri and Tammi. God, didn't you and your husband have any more imagination than that?"

No, Della thought. We each had too much imagination. Tammi and Terri were simply the names we finally could agree on. The names of compromise.

"You know something?" Chuckie raised his voice. "Now that I know where they live, I could drive over there in a while and say howdy. They wouldn't know a thing about what was going on, about what happened to their mom while she was out at the mall."

Oh God! thought Della.

"You want me to pass on any messages?"

"You little bastard!" She cried it out without thinking.

"Touchy, huh?" Chuckie slopped across the wet snow in her direction. "Come on out of the trees, Della-honey."

Della said nothing. She crouched behind a deadfall of brush and dead limbs. She was perfectly still.

Chuckie stood equally still, not more than twenty feet away. He stared directly at her hiding place, as though he could see through the night and brush. "Listen," he said. "This is getting real, you know, *boring*." He waited. "We could be out here all night, you know? All my buddies are gone now, and it's thanks to you, lady. Who the hell you think you are, Clint Eastwood?"

Della assumed that was a rhetorical question.

Chuckie hawked deep in his throat and spat on the ground. He rubbed the base of his throat gingerly with a free hand. "You hurt me, Della-honey. I think you busted my collarbone." He giggled. "But I don't hold grudges. In fact—" He paused contemplatively. "Listen now, I've got an idea. You know about droogs? You know, like in that movie?"

Clockwork Orange, she thought. Della didn't respond.

"Ending was stupid, but the start was pretty cool." Chuckie's personality seemed to have mutated into a manic stage. "Well, me droogs is all gone. I need a new gang, and you're real good, Dellahoney. I want you should join me."

"Give me a break," said Della in the darkness.

"No, really," Chuckie said. "You're a born killer. I can tell. You and me, we'd be perfect. We'll blow this popsicle stand and have some real fun. Whaddaya say?"

He's serious, she thought. There was a ring of complete honesty in his voice. She floundered for some answer. "I've got kids," she said.

"We'll take 'em along," said Chuckie. "I like kids, always

took care of my brothers and sisters." He paused. "Listen, I'll bet you're on the outs with your old man."

Della said nothing. It would be like running away to be a pirate.

Wouldn't it?

Chuckie hawked and spat again. "Yeah, I figured. When we pick up your kids, we can waste him. You like that? I can do it, or you can. Your choice."

You're crazy, she thought. "*I* want to," she found herself saying aloud.

"So come out and we'll talk about it."

"You'll kill me."

"Hey," he said, "I'll kill you if you *don't* come out. I got the light and the gun, remember? This way we can learn to trust each other right from the start. I won't kill you. I won't do nothing. Just talk."

"Okay." Why not, she thought. Sooner or later, he'll find his way in here and put the gun in my mouth and—Della stood up. —but maybe, just maybe—Agony lanced through her knees.

Chuckie cocked his head, staring her way. "Leave the tools."

"I already did. The ones I didn't use."

"Yeah," said Chuckie. "The ones you used, you used real good." He lowered the beam of the flashlight. "Here you go. I don't want you stumbling and falling and maybe breaking your neck."

Della stepped around the deadfall and slowly walked toward him. His hands were at his sides. She couldn't see if he was holding the gun. She stopped when she was a few feet away.

"Hell of a night, huh?" said Chuckie. "It'll be really good to go inside where it's warm and get some coffee." He held the flashlight so that the beam speared into the sky between them.

Della could make out his thin, pain-pinched features. She imagined he could see hers. "I was only going out to the mall for a few things," she said.

Chuckie laughed. "Shit happens."

"What now?" Della said.

"Time for the horror show." His teeth showed ferally as his lips drew back in a smile. "Guess maybe I sort of fibbed." He brought up his hand, glinting of metal.

"That's what I thought," she said, feeling a cold and distant sense of loss. "Huey, there, going to help?" She nodded to a point past his shoulder.

"Huey?" Chuckie looked puzzled just for a second as he glanced to the side. "Huey's—"

Della leapt with all the spring left in her legs. Her fingers closed around his wrist and the hand with the gun. "Christ!" Chuckie screamed, as her shoulder crashed against the spongy place where his broken collarbone pushed out against the skin.

They tumbled on the December ground, Chuckie underneath, Della wrapping her legs around him as though pulling a lover tight. She burrowed her chin into the area of his collarbone and he screamed again. Kenneth had always joked about the sharpness of her chin.

The gun went off. The flash was blinding, the report hurt her ears. Wet snow plumped down from the overhanging pine branches, a large chunk plopping into Chuckie's wide-open mouth. He started to choke.

Then the pistol was in Della's hands. She pulled back from him, getting to her feet, back-pedaling furiously to get out of his reach. She stared down at him along the blued-steel barrel. The pirate captain struggled to his knees.

"Back to the original deal," he said. "Okay?"

I wish, she almost said. Della pulled the trigger. Again. And again.

"Where the hell have you been?" said Kenneth as she closed the front door behind her. "You've been gone for close to three hours." He inspected her more closely. "Della, honey, are you all right?"

"Don't call me that," she said. "Please." She had hoped she would look better, more normal. Unruffled. Once Della had pulled the Subaru up to the drive beside the house, she had spent several minutes using spit and Kleenex trying to fix her mascara. Such makeup as she'd had along was in her handbag, and she had no idea where that was. Probably the police had it; three cruisers with lights flashing had passed her, going the other way, as she was driving north of Southeast Plaza.

"Your clothes." Kenneth gestured. He stood where he was.

Della looked down at herself. She'd tried to wash off the mud, using snow and a rag from the trunk. There was blood too, some of it Chuckie's, the rest doubtless from Vinh and Tomas.

"Honey, was there an accident?"

She had looked at the driver's side of the Subaru for a long minute after getting home. At least the car drove; it must just have been flooded before. But the insurance company wouldn't be happy. The entire side would need a new paint job.

"Sort of," she said.

"Are you hurt?"

To top it all off, she had felt the slow stickiness between her legs as she'd come up the walk. Terrific. She could hardly wait for the cramps to intensify.

"Hurt?" She shook her head. No. "How are the twins?"

"Oh, they're in bed. I checked a half hour ago. They're asleep."

"Good." Della heard sirens in the distance, getting louder, nearing the neighborhood. Probably the police had found her driver's license in Chuckie's pocket. She'd forgotten that.

"So," said Kenneth. It was obvious to Della that he didn't know at this point whether to be angry, solicitous or funny. "What'd you bring me from the mall?"

Della's right hand was nestled in her jacket pocket. She felt the solid bulk, the cool grip of the pistol.

Outside, the volume of sirens increased.

She touched the trigger. She withdrew her hand from the pocket and aimed the pistol at Kenneth. He looked back at her strangely.

The sirens went past. Through the window, Della caught a glimpse of a speeding ambulance. The sound Dopplered down to a silence as distant as the dream that flashed through her head.

Della pulled the trigger and the click seemed to echo through the entire house.

Shocked, Kenneth stared at the barrel of the gun, then up at her eyes.

It was okay. She'd counted the shots. Just like in the movies.

"I think," Della said to her husband, "that we need to talk."

The Murderer Chooses Sterility

BRADLEY DENTON

Introduction

In 1988, when Bradley Denton wrote from the point of view of a serial killer as a sympathetic character (or at least a character worth understanding), the entire concept was shocking. Now, after eight seasons of Dexter *with a ninth on the way, the concept seems almost quaint.*

Dexter *was based on a 2004 novel by Jeff Lindsay, who was publishing in the 1990s. I often wonder if he had read* Blackburn *(whom I find to be a much more appealing character than Dexter ever was).*

In the years since his first appearance in Pulphouse: A Hardback Magazine, *Brad has published several novels and has won the World Fantasy Award, the John W. Campbell Award, and Theodore Sturgeon Award, as well as being nominated for the Hugo, Nebula, Bram Stoker, and Edgar awards.*

Even if Blackburn isn't as shocking as he was in his early days, he's still a well drawn and very memorable character. After you read the story, you really should pick up the novel and its sequel.

Introduction

The Murderer Chooses Sterility

Bradley Denton

On the day after he killed his eleventh man, Blackburn decided
to have a vasectomy. That was because the Monday *Kansas City
Times* reported that the victim had been a father of four. Blackburn didn't enjoy reading it. He wished that he had stayed
behind the grill instead of taking his morning break.

It wasn't that he regretted what he had done. Late Sunday,
Number Eleven had run over a dog and had made a hash mark
in the air with his finger, so Blackburn had driven after him and
killed him at the next red light. It had been quick—one .357
bullet through the side window, and the light had changed.
Blackburn had rolled up his own window and driven on. No one
had seen. Kansas City was dead on Sunday nights.

Number Eleven had deserved what he had gotten, but
Blackburn thought it sad that the man had fathered four children who would now be warped by his cruelty in life and his
ugly death. With that thought, Blackburn realized that he
himself would not make an exemplary father and that he might
die an ugly death of his own.

After his experience with Dolores (whose paramour he had
thrown off the Golden Gate Bridge), he doubted that he would
ever take another wife. But he had a sex drive as strong as that

of any other twentyfour-year-old man, and women found his sandy hair and blue eyes attractive, so there would be girlfriends and one-nighters. He could not allow himself to impregnate them.

Paying for the operation might be a problem. Upon arriving in Kansas City in September, he had spent most of his cash on documents identifying him as Arthur B. Cameron, and the rest on a scabrous 1970 Dart. He had then landed his job at Bucky's Burgers, but in two months of work, he had saved only fifty dollars. He would have to find a clinic that performed cheap sterilizations.

During his afternoon break, he went into Bucky's office and looked through the Yellow Pages. He found what he needed under the heading of "Birth Control":

Responsible Reproduction of Kansas City
  Pregnancy Testing
  Birth Control/Family Planning
  Abortion Counseling and Services
  Vasectomies
  Fees Scaled to Income
  Open Noon to 10:00 P.M. Weekdays

The ad was followed by a telephone number and a midtown address. Blackburn's one-room basement apartment had no phone, and he didn't want to call from Bucky's, so he decided to visit Responsible Reproduction after work. He spent the rest of the afternoon in a state of anticipation, knowing that he was about to give a great gift to the world.

———

Stinking of deep-fryer grease, Blackburn pushed open a glass door embedded with wire mesh and found himself in a room illuminated by fluorescent tubes. Plastic chairs lined the walls. Most were occupied by women, a few of whom clutched the hands of nervous men. Three toddlers sat on the linoleum floor playing with G.I. Joe dolls. An odor of medicine mixed with Blackburn's own smell.

He approached a middle-aged woman who sat at a desk beside a doorway. A sign on the desk read *Ellen Duncan.* "Ms. Duncan," Blackburn said, "my name is Arthur Cameron. I want a vasectomy."

Ms. Duncan opened a drawer and brought out a pamphlet that she pushed across to him. It was entitled *Facts to Consider About Vasectomy (Male Sterilization).*

Blackburn took the pamphlet and gave it a glance. "Thank you," he said, "but I've considered the facts, and I've decided to have the operation. Could you tell me how much it will cost?"

Ms. Duncan frowned. "Our urologists charge Responsible Reproduction a hundred and ninety-five dollars. The amount that we pass on to the patient varies according to what he can afford." She paused. "Pardon me for asking, but have you discussed this with your spouse?"

"I'm not married."

"Are you in a long-term relationship?"

"No."

"Have you any children?"

"No." Blackburn wondered what these questions had to do with anything.

"Mr. Cameron," Ms. Duncan said, "our mission is to make family planning services available to those who couldn't afford them otherwise. We provide vasectomies to men who have consulted with their partners, whose families are complete, and whose incomes must support those families. We prefer that single men who have fathered no children see private physicians...."

A woman in a white smock appeared in the doorway. "Melissa," she called. "We're ready."

Across the room, a girl of sixteen or seventeen stood up. As she stepped around the children, she trembled.

"...but, in any case, you should read the pamphlet," Ms. Duncan was saying. She opened the drawer again and brought out a sheet of paper. "Then I hope you'll contact one of the physicians on this list." She put the list on the desk and looked at Blackburn as if she expected him to take it and leave.

He watched the girl named Melissa disappear down a hall.

"Why is she going back there?" he asked.

Ms. Duncan stared. "That's none of your business."

Blackburn stared back. "Does she have a family? Must her income support it? Did she consult her partner?"

Ms. Duncan's face flushed. "Please leave."

"Why?"

"Because I don't think you're here for information. I think you're one of those who stand outside and shout horrible things at the people who come to us for help. You're here to harass us."

Blackburn shook his head. "No. I'm here because I don't want kids. I have no partner to consult, but since I work as a short-order cook, I also have no savings account or health insurance."

Ms. Duncan studied him. "All right," she said, picking up a pen and poising it over a calendar. "You'll have to meet with our staff counselor."

"I don't need—"

"It's required. The discussion will deal with your reasons for this decision and with the nature of the procedure. Your cost will be calculated then." She looked at the calendar. "Could you come back tomorrow at 5:45?"

"I'll be here."

"I'm glad I was able to help you," Ms. Duncan said.

Blackburn was glad, too. When Ms. Duncan had begun asking her irritating questions, he had decided to kill her if she turned him away. He had never killed a woman before, and he had not been happy at the prospect.

———

The sun had gone down, and the air was cold. As Blackburn left the building, he put his hands into the side pockets of his jean jacket and gazed at the concrete walk. He didn't see the people who blocked his way until he was almost upon them. They hadn't been there when he'd arrived.

There were eight of them, clustered beside the drive that led to the clinic parking lot. Each held a burning candle in one hand and a handmade sign in the other. The letters shone in the glare of the streetlights.

Blackburn stopped and read the signs. GOD COUNTS THE CHILDREN, said one. SAVE THE UNBORN, said another. ABORTION IS MURDER, said a third.

A man stepped out of the cluster and asked, "Have you come from in there?" He pointed with his candle, and the flame faltered. "There where they butcher babies?"

"I've just been inside," Blackburn said, "but I don't know anything about any butchering."

A slender woman joined the man. She was dressed in a gray coal with matching gloves, muffler, and cap. Her eyes and lips gleamed with reflections of her candle flame. Wisps of brown hair quivered beneath the edge of her cap.

"If you've been in there, you know about it," she said. Her voice had a rich timbre, but was hoarse. "They do abortions."

"They didn't do one to me," Blackburn said. "Now, please, let me pass. My car is across the street."

"So why are you here?" the woman demanded. "Did you drop off your girlfriend so she could let them kill your baby? Or —" The flames in her eyes brightened. "Or have you killed babies yourself? Are you going to a home paid for with the flesh of infants?"

Blackburn had heard enough. These people were lucky that after his close call with Ms. Duncan, he didn't feel much like killing anyone tonight. He strode forward.

The man who had confronted him jumped aside, and the cluster of six did likewise. The woman in gray stayed where she was.

Blackburn stopped again to decide whether to shoulder his way past her or to try to go around.

The woman dropped her candle and reached into a pocket, bringing out a vial filled with dark liquid. She pulled out the stopper with her teeth (perfect teeth, Blackburn saw; white, smooth), then spat it out and screamed *"Murderer!"* She snapped the vial toward Blackburn as if it were the handle of a whip.

The liquid hit him in the face and got into his left eye and his mouth. He took his hands from his jacket pockets, and as he rubbed his eye, he tasted what was on his tongue: Blood. Cow's blood, pig's blood, maybe even blood that the woman had drawn from her own veins.

She remained before him, holding the vial like a weapon. It was not empty.

Blackburn took a step. The woman stood her ground. He reached out and plucked the vial from her glove, raised it to his lips, and drank. When the blood stopped flowing, he put his tongue inside and cleaned the glass.

Then he dropped the vial to the sidewalk and crushed it under his foot. The edge of his shoe caught the discarded candle as well, flattening it.

The woman gaped al him.

Blackburn walked around her and crossed the street to his car. Once inside, he turned on the interior light and examined the smears on his fingers. He almost reached for his Colt Python, which was nestled under the seal, but did not. He was calling it even with the woman in gray.

———

When he returned the next evening, the protesters were pacing, their breath wafting in faint clouds. He parked the Dart where he had the day before and walked across, but they ignored him as he passed. Inside, Ms. Duncan gave him a personal information and medical history form to fill out, and when he had completed it (having lied where necessary she led him to a cubicle where the staff counselor, a black man in his mid-thirties, was waiting. Ms. Duncan introduced the counselor as Lawrence Tatum.

"Call me Larry," Tatum said as Ms. Duncan left. He was sitting at a desk covered with a jumble of books, pamphlets, and folders. "I'll take that data sheet off your hands."

Blackburn handed him the form and sat down. The desk was against the wall, so the two men faced each other with nothing between them.

Tatum examined the form, then looked up and asked, "What happens if you decide to get married, your wife-to-be wants kids, and you've had your balls disconnected?"

Blackburn tried to imagine the situation, but the only wife-to-be he could picture was Dolores, she of the perpetual white bikini patches. "I won't be a father," he said, remembering how his own father had shot his dog and then pushed his face into the dirt for crying. "Any woman who knew me and still wanted to have children by me would make a poor wife."

"A vasectomy is permanent, Arthur. What if you turn thirty and all of a sudden, *blam*, you want to be a daddy?"

Blackburn doubted that he would live to be thirty, but he considered the question anyway. "That'll be tough shit for me, I guess," he said.

Tatum wrote on the form. "Okay. Let's talk about what'll happen during the operation, and then Duncan can schedule you for surgery."

Blackburn was surprised. "That's it?"

"For you it is. Couples take longer." Tatum began to rummage through the mess on his desk. "Besides, I figure that any guy who would be sterilized without understanding the consequences is a guy who shouldn't be spreading his dumb-ass genes around anyway."

It was the most honest statement Blackburn had ever heard. He liked Tatum.

Tatum found a card with a diagram of male genitalia and held it up. "You'll be given two shots of local anesthetic in the scrotum, one on either side of the base of the penis." He pointed with his pen. "After they take effect, the doctor will make a vertical incision midway between the vas deferens tubes. He'll pull one vas over to the incision, put a permanent clamp on it, and cut away a section. Then he'll repeal the procedure for the other side and close the incision with a few self-dissolving stitches. The whole thing takes about twenty minutes. Any questions?"

Blackburn stood. "How much will it cost?"

Tatum glanced at the form. "You'll need to bring a money order or cashier's check for ninety bucks." He picked up a telephone receiver and punched a button. "Ellen? When Mr. Cameron comes out, could you arrange the pre-vasectomy sample and schedule him for surgery? Thanks."

"What's a pre-vasectomy sample?" Blackburn asked.

"Semen specimen," Tatum said, hanging up the phone. "You'll need to take it to a medical lab within a half hour of ejaculation. We do the post-op sperm counts here, because then it doesn't matter whether we find the sperm alive or dead, only that we don't find any. For this one, though, we need a live count. You never know—maybe you won't have any."

"What are the odds of that?"

Tatum chuckled. "About the same as the odds of the Royals winning the Series next year. If you don't hear from us before your surgery date, assume that your count's in the normal range."

Blackburn thanked him and went out to Ms. Duncan, who gave him the address of the lab and told him to deliver his sample on Thursday morning. She also told him that his surgery would take place in one week, at 5:20 p.m.

"Soon," he said. "That's good."

"Every Tuesday," Ms. Duncan said. "There are two underway upstairs right now."

"Could I observe?"

Ms. Duncan said that she didn't think so. Then she gave him two instruction sheets and a baggie containing a single-bladed, blue plastic safety razor. The first instruction sheet told him what it was for.

Before going to the Dart, Blackburn stopped among the protesters and spoke to the woman in gray. "You have the wrong night. There's no baby-butchering today."

"I suppose you call it 'choice,'" she said.

Blackburn smiled. "No. Tonight it's 'crotch-cutting.' Or maybe 'scrotum-slicing.'"

"I can have you arrested for obscenity," the woman said.

Blackburn laughed and crossed the street. As he unlocked his car, he heard footsteps on the asphalt. Turning, he saw that the woman in gray had followed him. She had left her sign and candle on the sidewalk.

"Are you going to throw more blood?" Blackburn asked as she drew close.

The planes of her face seemed frozen. "You already have so much on you that it'll never wash off."

"Yet blood washes away sin."

"What would you know about that?"

He knew plenty, but instead of telling her so, he said, "I'm not an abortionist."

"It doesn't matter. If you work there, if you're *in* there, you're one of them. Condoning it is the same as doing it. It's evil."

"So why come over here? Shouldn't you be afraid of evil?"

She tilted her head. "I need to understand you if I'm going to fight you. How can you believe in what you do, and *do* what you do?"

For a moment, the sureness of her tone made Blackburn fear that she knew who he was, and knew the things he really had done. Then he remembered that she didn't even know him as Arthur Cameron, let alone as James Blackburn.

"You're wrong about me," he said. "In fact, I'm making sure that I'll never be the cause of what you're fighting." He look the baggie containing the plastic razor from his jacket. "This is to shave the hair off my scrotum. I'm having a vasectomy next week."

The planes of the woman's face crumpled, and she spun and stumbled into the street. A car was coming fast and would have hit her, but Blackburn pulled her back.

He was startled at what he had done. He didn't save people from themselves. He left people alone...unless they angered him, in which case he either punished them if the offense was slight, or killed them if it was great.

In the past seven years, the only exception to this rule had been that he had not killed Dolores.

The woman in gray clawed at his hands until he released her, and she rushed into the street again.

"Could I have that back?" Blackburn called.

She stopped. Her right hand was clutching the baggied razor.

She dropped it and ran to her fellow protesters.

Blackburn retrieved the razor, got into the Dart, and drove to his. apartment. All that night, the woman in gray filled his thoughts. He was afraid that he might be in love with her.

On Wednesday, Blackburn worked twelve hours al Bucky's. He needed the money.

On Thursday morning, he ejaculated into an empty breath-mint box and look it to the medical lab. He was embarrassed, not because he was delivering his own fresh semen, but because he had conjured up the ghost of the woman in gray to produce it. She had thrown blood on him, and then they had rolled together, each staining the other.

After a ten-hour shift behind the grill, he drove to Responsible Reproduction. The woman and her friends were there, but none of them seemed to recognize his car. He parked a short distance down the block, and for the next hour he watched them shout at everyone who went in and out of the building. The voice of the woman in gray rose above the rest.

On Friday night, after cashing his paycheck, he approached the clinic from the opposite direction and parked across the street from where he had the night before. He watched longer this time. At nine-thirty, the protesters blew out their candles and stacked their signs in a station wagon. Blackburn slouched low as they went to their cars.

The woman in gray crossed the street alone to a maroon Nova. When it left the curb, Blackburn followed.

He lost the Nova in traffic on the city's east side, but spotted it as he drove past a side street. It was parked under a streetlight, and the woman was standing on the porch of a small house. Blackburn pulled over and adjusted his rearview mirror so that he could see her. A light came on in the house, glowing yellow through the shades, and the door opened. A thin, backlit figure handed the woman something, and the door closed.

The woman returned to her car carrying bunches of red roses, their stems wrapped in green florist's paper. She cradled them as if she were carrying a child, but when she reached the Nova, she put them into the trunk.

Blackburn followed her again as she drove away. She went far west, into Kansas, but he didn't lose her.

The Nova stopped in the parking lot of an apartment complex in Mission, and Blackburn watched as the woman left her car and entered the complex through a security gate. A bank of mailboxes filled the wall beside the gate, so if he had known her name, he could have discovered her apartment number. But he didn't know her name.

He went to his own apartment and stayed up listening to the radio. The figure who had given the roses to the woman had looked male, but he was not her lover, Blackburn decided. She hadn't gone into his house, and she had left the flowers in the trunk of her car. At most, he was a friend. A friend with roses.

───────

Blackburn worked another ten-hour shift on Saturday, then drove past Responsible Reproduction. The lights were on, but there were only five protesters outside. The woman in gray was not among them. In bed that night, Blackburn lay awake wondering if she had abandoned her post because she had a date.

The next evening, there were no protesters at all. The street was empty, the clinic dark. Sunday in Kansas City.

He went to the apartment complex in Mission, thinking of breaking into the woman's car to find its registration slip and discover her name, but the Nova wasn't in the lot. He wished that he'd had the idea two nights ago.

Shivering and dozing, he waited for her to return. Once he dreamed of shooting a backlit figure, and awoke at the Python's report.

The Nova didn't appear, so Blackburn left at dawn and drove to the house of the roses. The woman's car wasn't there either, but he parked the Dart and watched the house until a skinny man who wore glasses came out and drove away in a Pinto.

Blackburn walked up to the porch and saw that the name on

the mailbox was "R. Petersen." He pressed the button beside the door and heard the bell ring. Inside, a dog barked. Blackburn pressed the button again, and the dog kept barking. No one came to the door.

Blackburn went to work. While on his mid-morning break, he read in the *Times* that a pipe bomb had exploded at Responsible Reproduction during the night. It had been set off outside the front door.

The police suspected that the bomber's intent had been to cause minor building damage, but the explosion had done more than that. A counselor named Lawrence Tatum had been doing paperwork in an inner office, and the police speculated that he had heard a noise and investigated.

They had found him in the waiting room with pieces of glass in his flesh. They thought that he had been starting to open the door when the bomb had gone off.

At press time, Tatum was in critical condition at St. Luke's. He had not regained consciousness. The police had no suspects. Ellen Duncan of Responsible Reproduction had announced that the clinic would continue its usual services.

After work, Blackburn bought a six-pack and a *Star,* which said that Tatum was still alive. The police had questioned some people, but they still had no suspects.

Blackburn went to his apartment. Five beers later, he was able to sleep.

———

On Tuesday, Blackburn left Bucky's at mid-afternoon. He stopped at a branch post office and bought a ninety-dollar money order.

At his apartment, he took off his work clothes and showered. Then he sat on the edge of the bathtub, soaped his scrotum, and shaved with the blue razor. It was a slow process because his testicles kept drawing up, but he persevered. His only alternative was to use his electric.

By the time he had dressed, it was five o'clock. He took the money order and the razor and drove to Responsible Reproduction.

More than thirty protesters were pacing the sidewalk when he arrived, and there were so many cars along the curbs that he had to park almost two blocks away. As he started to walk to the clinic, he saw the woman in gray emerge from a van with six others. He waved to her.

He had almost reached the building when he realized that he had left his money order m the Dart. He ran back to get it, and the woman and some of her companions stepped off the sidewalk to avoid him.

"Tonight I do it!" he shouted as he ran past. The woman averted her eyes.

When he reached his car, he glimpsed a bit of color on the pavement and squatted to pick it up. It was a rose petal. The edges were black and curled, but the center was bright. He crushed and dropped it, then grabbed the money order and hurried back to Responsible Reproduction. Several protesters yelled at him, but the woman in gray was quiet.

The glass-and-wire-mesh door was gone, and in its place was a slab of plywood with a handle. Blackburn opened it and went inside.

———

He lay on a padded table that was covered with blue paper. His naked buttocks rested on a pad of the stuff.

His knees were supported by saddle-shaped pieces of plastic atop metal posts, and his feet hung in the air, chilling. He wished that he had left his socks on.

The crew-cut medical assistant took a spray bottle from a counter and bathed Blackburn's crotch in a cold mist. Blackburn gasped. "Antiseptic," the assistant said. He returned to the counter, opened a packet, and pulled out another pad of blue paper. When he unfolded it, a hole appeared in its center. He laid it over Blackburn's crotch and pressed down so that the scrotum pushed up through the hole. The upper half of the paper became a curtain between Blackburn's thighs.

"Doctor'll be in soon," the assistant said, and left.

Blackburn lowered his head and stared up. Above him, attached to the ceiling with thumbtacks, was a poster of a kitten clutching a knot in midair. Underneath the kitten were the words,

When you've reached the end of your rope, HANG ON!

Blackburn wanted to tear it down. He wasn't in the mood for cute bullshit.

Then, as the antiseptic evaporated and made his testicles feel as if they were packed in ice, it occurred to him that this room was used for vasectomies only on Tuesday evenings. On other evenings, it was used for other things.

He was lying on a table where women had lain for abortions.

He thought of the girl named Melissa. Would the kitten have meant something to her, or would she have thought it as stupid as he did?

The assistant returned with the doctor, who was wearing a green smock over chinos. The doctor had thinning hair and looked about forty. "Let's get to it," he said.

Blackburn raised his head and watched as the assistant brought a cart and a stool to the foot of the table. When the cloth over the cart was removed, he saw a syringe and an array of stainless-steel instruments.

"You'll be more comfortable if you keep your head relaxed," the doctor said.

Blackburn lowered his head again, but he was no more comfortable. With peripheral vision, he saw the assistant pick up the spray bottle again. A second cold mist hit his scrotum and hissed against the blue paper. The assistant placed the bottle on the cart, then opened a package of latex gloves and helped the doctor put them on.

The doctor nudged the stool with his foot and sat down between Blackburn's legs. Blackburn could see his face, but his hands were hidden behind the blue paper.

"I'll check on the other guy," the assistant said. "The jerk showed up half-shaved." He left the room.

The doctor grasped Blackburn's testicles, pulled them away from the body, and began rolling the skin above the right testicle between his thumb and forefinger. Blackburn's calf muscles contracted, and his feet cramped. He had to grab the edges of the table to hold himself down.

"I have to find the vas," the doctor said.

Blackburn clenched his teeth and glared at the kitten.

"Got it," the doctor said. "Now I'll give you the first shot of anesthetic. It's procaine hydrochloride, like the Novocain you get at the dentist's."

Blackburn had been to a dentist twice, and both times he had suffered. Novocain did not work well on him.

"Here it comes, in the top right side," the doctor said. "It'll feel like a bee sting."

It was worse than that. Blackburn's back arched, and his thumbs tore through the paper covering the table. He strained to keep from pulling his legs off the posts and kicking the doctor in the face.

The needle withdrew, and the doctor began manipulating the left side as he had the right. "One more," he said, and the needle went in. Sweat trickled into Blackburn's ears.

"Try to hold still," the doctor said.

The needle withdrew again. Blackburn lay still for a moment, then raised his head to see what was happening.

The doctor was looking up at his face. "How old are you?" he asked.

"Twenty-four."

"Ah. How many children do you have?"

Blackburn wanted to hurt him. "None. So what?"

"Ah," the doctor said again. He shifted on the stool, and his right hand appeared above the blue curtain. It held a blood..- smeared scalpel.

"What does 'ah' mean?" Blackburn asked.

The doctor laid the scalpel on the cart and picked up another instrument, moving it behind the paper before Black- burn could see what it looked like.

"Never mind," the doctor said, looking down at his work again. "I'm going to pull the right vas over to the incision now. You might feel a slight tug."

It was as if a vein in Blackburn's abdomen were being yanked out through the scrotum. Blackburn rose on his elbows.

"*Please* hold still," the doctor said.

Blackburn wished that he could feel justified in killing the doctor, but he knew that he couldn't. He had asked for this.

Much later, the doctor said, "You seemed to experience some discomfort, so I'll give you another shot before I do the left vas. It won't be as bad this time, because you're already some- what deadened."

The kitten was a yellow blur. Blackburn tried to brace himself, but it didn't help. The woman in gray, he thought, had better appreciate this.

———

When the stitched wound was covered with gauze, Blackburn got down from the table and put on his clothes and jacket. He couldn't feel the pressure of the athletic supporter, or of his jeans. It was as if he had no genitals.

The doctor gave him a prescription for tetracycline and left the room. Blackburn started to leave as well, but paused at the foot of the table. He was surprised at how much the blue paper on which he had lain was blackened.

The assistant came in with a trash bag and began taking up the paper. He glanced at Blackburn and said, "You're finished, aren't you?"

Blackburn went out. Downstairs, Ms. Duncan smiled at him. "We'll see you in a few weeks for your first sperm check, Mr. Cameron."

"Right." He moved toward the plywood door.

"Oh, you might like to know that I just called the hospital about Larry Tatum," Ms. Duncan said. "He'll lose two fingers and maybe his right eye, but he's out of danger and joking about the whole thing."

"That's good," Blackburn said, and left.

Outside, among the protesters, he stopped before the woman in gray. "I'm sterile," he said.

"Get away from me." She was surrounded by candles, and her face wavered between dark and light.

Blackburn looked back at the clinic. "A bomb went off here two nights ago. A person was hurt."

"That's what they'd like us to think," the woman said, "but it's a lie to make it look as if *we're* in the wrong. If we stopped marching, we'd be giving in to that lie."

Blackburn's wound began to throb. "I admire your strength," he said, and walked on to the Dart. Each step hurt more.

———

The van wouldn't bring the woman home for at least two more hours, and no one approached Blackburn as he opened the trunk of the maroon Nova. When he was finished, there would be no evidence that he had done it. Trunks were easy.

A bulb came on as the lid lifted, and a heavy scent reminded Blackburn of compost and funerals. In addition to a tire and a jack, the trunk contained three bunches of wilted roses.

The paper around one bunch was loose, and a few flowers had fallen free. Blackburn picked up this bunch and pressed his face into the dead petals, then put it down and reached for another. This one was heavier, so he left it on the floor of the trunk and unwrapped it.

Among the rose stems was a twelve-by-two-inch iron pipe that was capped at both ends. A cord almost as long as the pipe hung from a hole in the center of one of the caps.

Blackburn picked up the pipe and shook it, listening to the rattle. He had used something similar once, so he knew that the pipe contained a stick of dynamite and a blasting cap. This was the simplest sort of pipe bomb, a bangalore torpedo. When he opened the third bunch of flowers, he found another.

His pulse was trying to break through his stitches, so he began to hurry. He unbuttoned a jacket pocket and took out the razor, dropped it, and stamped on it. He used the freed blade lo slice off half of each fuse.

After rewrapping the pipes into their flower bundles, he closed the trunk and gathered up the razor's plastic shards. On the way to the Dart, he dropped them into the gutter.

He had his prescription filled at an all-night pharmacy. Then he went to his apartment, took four aspirin, and lay in bed with an ice pack on his crotch. He couldn't sleep, so he read the "Instructions to Follow After a Vasectomy" sheet over and over.

Instruction #8 said that it would take from fifteen to thirty-five ejaculations to clear the sperm from his tubes. After fifteen ejaculations, he was to bring a specimen to Responsible Reproduction for examination.

Blackburn doubted that he would remain in Kansas City long enough to do that.

The name of the woman in gray, the next Monday's *Times* said, had been Leslie Bonner. She had shared her apartment with her mother.

She had placed her second bomb outside the door of an obstetrician/gynecologist's office in Overland Park. It had gone off when she was twelve feet away, and her head had hit the sidewalk when she fell.

Her car had been found nearby, with another bomb in the trunk. The police were investigating to discover the source of the dynamite.

Blackburn looked at the picture of Leslie Bonner for his entire morning break.

Either she hadn't noticed that the fuse on her second bomb was shorter than the one on her first, or she had thought that it didn't matter. She had trusted the maker. She had failed to understand the consequences.

No one had saved her from herself.

Blackburn dropped the newspaper into the garbage. He worked until the end of his usual shift and left Bucky's without cleaning the grill.

At his apartment, he gathered his possessions and put them into his duffel bag. Then he lay on the bed and waited for night.

She hadn't looked like a Leslie. If anything, Blackburn would have guessed her to be a Lisa, or a Lydia. Thinking about her, he started to have an erection, but the stitches pulled at his skin and stopped it.

At eleven o'clock, he went into the bathroom and examined his incision. The swelling was gone and the stitches were dissolving, but his scrotum was still bruised. He put a new gauze pad over the wound, pulled up his jeans, and took his duffel bag out to the Dart. The weight made him ache. He wasn't supposed to carry anything heavy yet.

He drove to the east side of the city and parked a few blocks from the house of the roses. He tucked the Python into the back waistband of his jeans so that it was hidden by his jacket, then walked the rest of the way. The street was quiet, the homes dark.

The house's shades were drawn, but there was a light on inside. As Blackburn stepped onto the porch, he heard the sound of televised laughter. R. Petersen was watching David Letterman.

Blackburn took the pieces of fuse from his pocket and tied them together. He lit one end with a match, then held the knot in his left hand while he took the Python into his right. He pressed the revolver's muzzle against the doorbell button.

When the door opened, he tossed the fuse inside. R. Petersen turned toward it, and Blackburn hit him behind the ear with the Python. Petersen fell.

Blackburn went inside and closed the door as Petersen crawled across the hardwood floor toward the fuse. Blackburn stepped around him and turned up the volume on the television set.

Petersen reached the fuse and slapped at it.

Blackburn took a pillow from a chair, pressed it over Petersen's head, and fired one round through it. The fuse sputtered out by itself. He found a roll of tens and twenties in a dresser drawer in the bedroom, and a half-grown, black-and-white mongrel pup in the kitchen. He found a box containing dynamite, blasting caps, crimpers, and fuse hidden among junk in the basement.

When he was ready to go, he carried the box outside and dumped it on the street. Then he returned to the house and lit the fuse he had looped around the living room. That done, he took the pup and left. The pup was heavier than she looked, and she squirmed. By the time Blackburn reached the Dart, he was sore and had to take aspirin.

He didn't think that the single stick of dynamite in Number Twelve's mouth would endanger the neighboring homes, but he stopped at a pay phone and called 911 anyway. He didn't know the house's exact address, but he told the dispatcher which street and block.

Then he drove north on 1-35. He would dump the Dart in Des Moines, acquire another car, and go on to Chicago. He had never been there.

"Chicago sound good?" he asked the pup.

The pup gnawed on the butt of the Python and growled. Blackburn was having trouble thinking of a good name for her.

Maybe he wouldn't give her one.

The Two-Headed Man

NANCY A. COLLINS

Introduction

I still remember the day I first read "The Two-Headed Man." I was sitting in my office at Pulphouse Publishing, while everyone around me wanted dinner. I finally had to get up and close the door, because, by gum, I was going to finish reading this story. I couldn't believe that Nancy was able to make it work.

"The Two-Headed Man" is one of the reasons the Hardback Magazine existed. Initially, the story sold to Playboy, *but the Powers That Be at the magazine decided that the story was "too odd" to publish.*

Not for us. We published it and it became one of the defining stories of our early years.

Nancy exploded onto the publishing scene with a revolutionary vampire novel called Sunglasses After Dark. *In the decades since, she's published more than fifteen novels, dozens of short stories, and for two years, she took over* Swamp Thing *for D.C. Comics. She's known as a Southern Gothic horror writer, but her work is more nuanced than that.*

She's always been daring and outrageous, as this early story shows.

The Two-Headed Man

Nancy A. Collins

It was going on midnight when the two-headed man walked into Kelly's Stop.

The short-order cook glanced up when the short burst of cold air rifled the newspaper spread across the Formica serving counter. The man stood in the diner's doorway, the fur-fringed hood of the parka casting his face in deep shadow. He tugged off his mittens and stuffed them into one pocket, flexing his fingers like a pianist before a recital.

"You're in luck, buddy," said the cook, refolding the newspaper. "We was just about ready to call it an early night."

The waitress stabbed out a cigarette and pivoted on her stool to get a better look at the stranger. She tugged at her blouse waist, causing her name, LOUISE, to twitch over her heart.

"Car had a flat...up the road..." came a voice from inside the shadow of the parka's hood. "We don't...have a spare..."

The cook shrugged, his back to the stranger. "Can't help you there, bub. Mike Keckhaver runs the Shell station down the road a piece, but he don't open up 'till tomorrow morning."

"Then we'll...have to wait."

"'We'?" Louise moved to the front window and peered out

59

between the neon Miller Hi-Life and Schlitz signs. The gravel parking lot fronting the diner was empty. "You got somebody with you, mister?"

"Yes...You could say that," answered the stranger as he unzipped the parka and tossed back the hood.

Louise gasped and clamped a hand over her mouth, smearing lipstick against her palm. The cook spun around to see what was going on, butcher knife in hand: late-night truck-stop robberies were not uncommon along Highway 65.

The stranger had two heads. One was where heads are supposed to be. And a damn fine one at that. It was the handsomest head Louise had ever seen this side of a TV screen. The stranger's hair was longish and curly and the color of winter wheat. It framed a face designed for a movie star—straight nose, strong and beardless chin, high cheekbones, and eyes bluer than Paul Newman's.

The second head looked over the stranger's left shoulder, perched on his collarbone like a parrot. It wasn't a deformed or even an unsightly head—just average. But its extreme proximity to such masculine perfection made it seem...repulsive. The second head was dark where the other was fair, brown-eyed where the first was blue. It regarded Louise with a distant, oddly disturbing intelligence then turned so its lips moved against it's fellow's left ear. The stranger laughed without much humor.

"Yeah, guess I *did* scare 'em some..." The stranger shrugged off his coat. "Sorry, didn't mean to startle you like that."

Now that the parka was all the way off they could see that the stranger really didn't have two heads. A padded leather harness, like those worn by professional hitchhikers, was strapped to his shoulders and midsection. But instead of a bed roll and an army surplus dufflebag, he carried a little man on his back.

The stranger seated himself on one of the stools, leaning slightly forward under the weight of his burden.

"What is he? A dwarf or somethin'?" The cook ignored the look Louise shot him.

The man did not seem at all insulted. "Nope. Human Worm."

"Huh?"

"Carl's got no arms...or legs."

"That so? Was he in Viet Nam?"

"No. Just born that way."

"How about that. Don't see that every day."

"No, you don't," he agreed amiably. The Human Worm leaned closer and whispered into his ear again. The stranger nodded. "Okay. Why not, long as we're here. We'll have two orders of bacon and eggs...one scrambled...one sunny-side up...two orders of toast...and two coffees. Got that?" The stranger pulled a cloth hankie out of his pants pocket and draped it over his left shoulder.

"Uh, yeah. Sure. Comin' right up."

"Name's Gary. This here's Carl," the stranger jerked a thumb to indicate his piggyback passenger.

"Pleased t'meetcha," the cook grunted.

Carl bobbed his head in silent acknowledgment.

Louise stood near the end of the serving counter, debating on whether she should try to talk to the handsome stranger with the freak tied to his back.

Talking to the various strangers that found their way into Kelly's Stop was one of the few perks the job had to offer. The trouble with the locals was that she knew what they were going to say before they even opened their mouths. She hated living in a pissant little town like Seven Devils. She envied the strangers she met; travelers from somewhere on their way to someplace. She liked to pretend that maybe one of them would be her long-awaited Dream Prince and take her away from Kelly's Stop— just like Ronald Coleman rescued Bette Davis in *Petrified Forest*. But if her Prince was going to put in an appearance, it was going to have to be pretty damn soon. Her tits were starting to sag and the laugh-lines at the corners of her eyes were threatening to become crow's feet.

She studied the two men as they waited to be served. It was sure as hell a *weird* set-up. But that face…Gary's face…was the one she'd pictured in her fantasies. It was the face of the Prince who would deliver her from a lifetime of bunions, corn plasters, varicose veins and cheap beer.

The more she thought about it, he wasn't really *that* strange. It was kind of sweet, really, the way he carried the crippled guy on his back. It wasn't that much different than pushing a wheelchair.

The cook plopped the eggs and bacon onto the grill, slammed twin slices of bread into the toaster and returned his attention to the spitting bacon.

"Louise! Get th' man his coffee, willya?" The command made her jump and she scurried over to the Bun-O-Matic coffee-maker.

"How you like it?" she asked, hoping she didn't sound shrill. Her hands were shaking. She took a deep breath before she poured.

"Black. Cream and sugar."

She slid the cups across the counter and located a sugar dispenser. She felt his eyes on her as she moved to get the cream from the cooler, but she wasn't sure which one of them was doing the looking.

Gary picked up the cup of black coffee with his left, blew on it a couple of times, then lifted it over his shoulder. Carl lowered his head and noisily sipped from the lip of the cup while Gary stirred his coffee with his right hand.

"Wow. Neat trick." She kicked herself the minute she said it. What a *hick* thing to say!

Gary shrugged, causing Carl to bounce slightly. "Helps if you're ambidextrous."

"Ambiwhat?"

"Carl says that's being good with both hands," he explained, gesturing with a piece of bacon. Carl leaned forward, grasping the proffered strip with surprisingly white, even teeth before bolting it down like a lizard.

Louise watched as Gary fed himself and his rider, both hands moving with unthinking grace. He acted as if it was as natural for him as breathing. Carl wiped his mouth and chin, shiny with grease and butter, on the napkin draped over his companion's shoulder. His eyes met Louise's and she hastily looked away.

There was something hot and alive in those eyes; something hungry and all too familiar. Her cheeks burned and she dropped a bouquet of clean flatware onto the floor.

"Look, mister, I'm gonna be closin' shop real soon. Like I said, the Shell station don't open 'till seven or eight. There's a motel up the road a bit, the Driftwood Inn. You shouldn't have no trouble findin' a place there. They're right off th' highway, so they're open all night. I'd give you a lift but, uh, my car's in the shop an' I live in town, so…" the cook fell silent and returned to cleaning his grill.

The two-headed man sat and drank coffee while Louise and her boss busied themselves with the ritual of closing. Louise mopped the floor faster than usual, trying not to look at the stranger and his freakish papoose.

"Well, lights out, folks," the cook announced with a forced smile. The two-headed man stood up and began shouldering themselves back into the parka. "Uh, look, Louise…Why don't you lock up for me, huh? Laurie's waitin' up on me and you know how she gets."

Louise certainly did. Laurie had had enough of waiting up for her husband three years back and joined the others who'd abandoned Seven Devils, Arkansas. She nodded and watched him flee the diner for the safety of a nonexistent wife.

Gary pulled the parka's hood over his head and zipped up. All she could see was his face—that achingly handsome face—with its baby-smooth jaw and electric blue eyes.

It was bitterly cold outside, their breath wreathing their heads. The hard frost had turned the highway into a strip of polished onyx. Gary stuffed his hands into his mittens, gave Louise a nod and a half-wave and began to walk away, the parking lot's gravel crunching under his bootheels. The lump under his parka stirred.

Do something, girl! Say something! don't just let him walk off!

"Hey, mister…er, misters!"

He turned to smile at her. She felt her bravado slip. *Dear God, what am I getting myself into?* But it was two in the morning and everyone in Choctaw County was asleep except for her and the blue-eyed stranger…and his traveling companion.

"I've got a place 'round back. It's not much, but it's warm. You're welcome to stay…I hate to think of you walking all the way to the motel and then it turn out to be full-up."

Gary stood there for a moment, his hands in his pockets and his head cocked to one side as if he was listening to something.

Then he smiled.

"We'd be delighted."

———

The frozen grass crunched gently under their feet. The dark bulk of Louise's trailer loomed ahead of them, resting on its bed of cinderblocks.

"Where are we…exactly? We've no real idea…."

"You're in Choctaw County."

"That's the name of this place?"

"No. Not really. This here's Seven Devils. Or its outskirts, at least. Not much to it, except that it's the county seat. This used to be a railroad town, back before the war. But now that everything's shipped by trucks, there ain't a whole lot left. What makes you want to drive around in this part of Arkansas in the first place? There's nothing down here but rice fields, bayous and broke farmers."

"We like the old highways…we meet much nicer people that way…"

Louise stopped to glance over her shoulder as she dug the house key from her coat pocket. Had it been Gary's voice she'd heard that time? All she could see was shadow inside the parka's hood. She stood on the cinderblock that served as her front stoop and fussed with her key-chain. She could hear him breathing at her elbow.

"Welcome to my humble abode! It ain't much, but it's home. It used to belong to the boss. I keep an eye on the place for him." Why was she so anxious? He certainly wasn't the first man she'd invited back to her trailer before. She'd known her share of truckers and salesmen and hitchhikers, tricked out in their elaborate backpacks. Some of them she'd even deluded herself into thinking might be her Prince in disguise.

Each time there had been the meeting of tongues, the grunts in the dark as groins slapped together, and the cool evaporation of sweat on naked flesh. Each time she woke up alone. Sometimes there'd be money on the dresser.

She flicked on the lights as she entered the trailer. The tiny kitchen and shoebox-sized den emerged from the darkness.

"Like I said, it ain't much."

He stood on the threshold, one hand on the doorknob. "It's nice, Louise."

She shivered at the sound of her name in his mouth. She moved into the living room, hoping for a chance to compose herself. She needed to think.

"Close the door! You're lettin' the cold air in!" her voice unnaturally chirpy.

Gary closed the door behind him. She felt a bit more secure, but she couldn't help notice how worn and tacky everything looked: the sofa, the dinette set, the easy chair… For a fleeting second she was overwhelmed by a desire to cry.

Gary removed his parka, carefully draping it over the back of the easychair. He was wearing faded denims and a flannel shirt and he was so beautiful it scared her to look at him. He was so perfect she could almost ignore the Human Worm strapped to his back.

"Get you a drink?"

"That would be…nice."

She hurried past him and back into the kitchen. She retrieved her bottle of Evan Williams and a couple of high ball glasses. She poured herself two fingers, knocked it back, then poured another two before preparing a drink for her guest. She returned to the living room—he was standing in the exact same spot—and handed Gary the glass.

"Skoal."

"Cheers," he replied, lifting the glass to Carl's lips.

While his partner drank, Gary's eyes met and held hers. "We know why you invited us here, Louise…"

Her heart began to beat funny, as if she'd been given a powerful but dangerous drug. She wanted this man, this gorgeous stranger. She wanted to feel his weight on her, pressing her into the mattress of her bed.

"…but there's one thing you ought to know before we get started…and that's Carl's got to go first."

She stood perfectly still for a second before the words her Dream Prince had spoken sank in. She was keenly aware of Carl's eyes watching her. Her face burned and her stomach balled itself into a fist. She felt as if she'd awakened from a dream to find herself trapped in the punchline from a dirty joke.

"What kind of pervert do you think I am?" The tightness in her throat pitched her voice ever higher.

"I don't think you're a pervert, Louise. I think you're a very sweet, very special lady. I didn't mean to hurt you." There was no cynicism in his voice. His tone was that of a child confused by the irrationality of adults.

She felt her anger fade. She gulped down the rest of her drink, hoping it would fan the fires of her indignation. "I expected something kinky out of you—like maybe letting th' little guy watch…But not, y'know…"

"I see."

Gary moved to retrieve his parka. Before she realized what she was doing, she grabbed his arm. She was astonished by the intensity of her reaction.

"No! Don't leave! Please…it's so lonely here…"

"Yes, it is lonely," he whispered. His eyes would not meet hers. "Go stand over there. By the sofa. Where we can see you."

Louise did as she was told. Everything seemed so far away, as if she was watching a movie through the wrong end of a pair of binoculars. Her arms and legs felt so fragile they might have been made of light and glass.

Carl whispered into Gary's ear. His eyes had grown sharp and alive while Gary's seemed to lose their focus.

"Take off your blouse. Please." The words came from someplace far away.

She hesitated, then her hands moved to the throat of her blouse. The buttons seemed cold and alien, designed to frustrate her fingers. One by one they surrendered until her shirtfront fell open, revealing pale flesh. She shrugged her shoulders and the blouse fell to the floor.

Carl once more whispered something to Gary, never taking his eyes off Louise. "The skirt. Take it off."

Her hands found the fastener at her waist. Plastic teeth purred on plastic zipper and her skirt dropped to the floor, a dark puddle at her ankles. She took a step forward, abandoning her clothes.

Carl murmured into Gary's ear. She unhooked her bra, revealing her breasts. Her skin was milky white and decorated by dark aureole. Her nipples were painfully erect and as hard as corn kernels.

On Carl's relayed command she skinned herself free of her pantyhose. When the cool air struck her damp pubic patch, her clitoris stirred.

Gary moved towards her, bringing Carl with him.

She gasped aloud when Gary's hands touched her breasts. His thumbs flicked expertly over her nipples, sending shudders of pleasure through her. Then one hand was between her legs, teasing her thatch and gently massaging her.

Louise felt her knees buckle and she grabbed hold of Gary's shoulders to keep from falling backwards. Her eyes opened and she found herself staring into Carl's dark, intense eyes. She felt a brief surge of shame that her orgasm had become a spectator event, then Gary worked a finger past her labia and sank it to the second joint. Louise groaned aloud and all thoughts of shame disappeared.

He moved swiftly and quietly, wrapping her in his powerful arms and lifting her bodily. She felt a different form of pleasure now, as if she was once more within her father's safe embrace.

He moved down the narrow hall, past the cramped bathroom alcove and into the tiny bedroom at the back of the trailer. He lowered her trembling body onto the bed, draping her legs over the edge of the mattress.

His left hand continued to trace delicate patterns along her exposed flesh while his right loosened the harness that held Carl in place. He only halted his exploration of her body when he moved to free his burden.

Louise saw that Carl was dressed in a flannel shirt identical to Gary's, except that the empty sleeves had been pinned up and the shirt tail folded back on itself and fastened shut, just like a diaper. Gary removed the shirt and Louise swore out loud.

Even on a normal man's body Carl's penis would have been unusually large. It stood red and erect against the thick dark hair of his belly. Louise was so taken aback she scarcely noticed the smooth lumps of flesh that should have been Carl's arms and legs.

Gary positioned Carl's naked torso between her spread thighs. His gaze met and held her own so intently Louise almost forgot the absurd perversity of what they were doing.

"We love you," said Gary and shoved Carl on top of her.

Louise cried out as Carl penetrated her. It had been a long time since she'd last been with a man, and she had never known one of such proportions. She involuntarily contracted her hips, taking him in deeper. Gary's right hand kneaded the flesh of her breasts. His left hand helped Carl move. She could also feel something warm and damp just below her breasts. She suddenly realized it was Carl's face.

Gary's face was closer to hers now, his eyes mirroring her heat. She snared a handful of his hair, drawing him closer. His mouth was warm and wet as he clumsily returned her kiss. She felt the quivering that signaled the approach of orgasm and her moans became cries, giving voice to an exquisite wounding. Her hips bucked wildly with each spasm, but Carl refused to be unseated.

As she lay dazed and gasping in her own sweat, she was dimly aware of him still working between her legs. Then there was a deep groan, muffled by her own flesh, and she felt him stiffen and then relax.

Louise rarely experienced orgasms during intercourse. She had been unprepared for such intensity; it was if Gary had stuck his finger in her brain and swirled everything around so she was no longer sure what she thought or knew.

No. Not Gary. Carl.

The thought made her catch her breath and she raised herself onto her elbows, staring down at the thing cradled between her thighs. Carl's face was still buried in her breast. She touched his hair and felt him start from the unexpected contact. It was the first time since their strange rut had begun that she'd acknowledged his presence.

She felt Gary watching her as she moved back further onto the bed. Carl remained curled at the foot of the mattress, his eyes fixed on her. Gary stood in the narrow space between the bed and the dresser, his hands at his side.

"What about you? Aren't you interested?" Her voice was

hoarse. Gary did not meet her gaze as he shifted his weight from foot to foot.

"What's the matter? Is it me?"

His head jerked up. "No! It's not you. You're fine. It's just…" He fell silent and looked to Carl, who nodded slightly.

Gary took a deep breath and loosened his belt buckle. His manner had changed completely. His movements had lost their previous grace. Biting his lower lip and tensing as if in anticipation of a blow, he dropped his pants.

Gary's sex organs were the size of a two year old child's. They lay exposed like fragile spring blossoms, his pubic area as smooth and hairless as his face. His eyes remained cast down.

Louise's lips twisted into a wry smile. She had willingly serviced a freak in order to please her long-awaited Prince, only to find him gelded. Yet all she could feel for the handsome near-man was sorrow.

"You poor thing. You poor, poor thing." She reached out and touched his hand, drawing him into the warmth of her arms. Surprised, Gary eagerly returned her embrace. To her own surprise, she reached down to pull Carl toward her. The three of them lay together on the bed like a nest of snakes, Louise gently caressing her lovers. After awhile Gary began to talk.

"I've known Carl since we were kids. My mama used to cook and clean for his folks and I kept Carl company. His mama and daddy were real rich; that's how they could afford to keep him home. At least his mama wanted him home. Carl's daddy drank a lot and used to say how it wasn't his fault in front of Carl. I knew how he felt. About having your daddy hate you because of the way you was born. Maybe that's why me and Carl made such good friends. You see, I can't read so good. And I'm really bad with math and things like that. My daddy got mad at my mama when they found out what was wrong with me and ran away. I never really went to school. When Carl was five, his daddy got real mad and started kickin' him. And Carl hadn't even done anything bad! He kicked Carl in the throat and they took him to the hospital. That's why Carl can't talk too good. But he's real smart! Smarter than most people with arms and legs! He knows a lot about history and math and important stuff like that. Carl tells me what to say and how to act and what to do so people don't know I've got something wrong with me. If people knew I wasn't smart they'd be even meaner to us." He exchanged a warm, brotherly smile with the silent man and squeezed him where his shoulder should have been. "Carl looks after me. I'm his arms and legs and voice and he's my brain and, you know." He blushed.

"You're lucky. Both of you. Not everyone is as…whole."

"But we're not!" He folded her hands inside his own. "Not really. That's why we've been traveling. We've been trying to find the last part of us. The part that will make us whole."

Louise did not know what to say to this, so she simply kissed him. Sometime later they fell asleep, Carl's torso curled between them like a dozing pet.

The alarm went off at eight-thirty, jarring Louise from a dreamless sleep. She lay there for a moment, staring at Gary then Carl. She should have felt soiled, but there was no indignation inside her. She gently shook Gary's beautiful naked shoulder.

"It's morning already. The filling station must be open by now. You can get your tire fixed."

"Yes." His voice sounded strangely hollow.

She got out of the rumpled bed, careful to keep from kicking Carl, and put on a housecoat. Now that it was daylight she felt embarrassed to be naked. She hurried into the kitchen and made coffee.

Gary emerged from the bedroom, dressed, with Carl once more harnessed to his back. She handed him two mugs, one black and one with cream and sugar, and watched, a faint smile on her lips, as they repeated their one-as-two act.

After they'd finished, Gary picked his parka up and laid it

across one arm. He glanced first at her then angled his head so that he was as close to face-to-face with his passenger as possible. After a moment's silent communion, he once more turned to look at her, and his eyes lost their focus. Carl's lips moved at his ear and Louise could hear the faint rasping of his ruined voice.

Gary spoke like a man reading back dictation.

"Louise...you're a wonderful woman...I know you're not attracted to me, that's understandable...but I see something in you that might, someday...respond to *me* too..."

As Gary continued his halting recitation, Louise's gaze moved from his face to Carl's. For the first time since she'd met them, she really looked at him. She studied his plain, everyday face and his brown eyes. As she listened the voice she heard was Carl's and she felt something inside her change.

"We'll stop back after we get the tire repaired...It's up to you...We shouldn't be more than an hour at the most. Please think about it."

Gary began to put his parka on, but before the jacket hid Carl completely she darted forward and kissed both of them. First Gary, and then, with great care, Carl. They paused for a second and then smiled.

Louise stood in the middle of the trailer, hugging herself against the morning cold, as she watched her lovers leave. Funny. She'd always imagined her Prince having blue eyes...

Savage Breasts

NINA KIRIKI HOFFMAN

Introduction

Nina Kiriki Hoffman's "Savage Breasts" is probably the iconic Pulp-house story. Everyone who reads this story remembers it. I can't imagine it appearing anywhere else. And perhaps the strangest thing about this story is that it feels weirdly plausible.

In the years before its publication in Pulphouse, "Savage Breasts" had already reached cult status. Nina wrote the story at the Clarion Writers Workshop, which was then held at Michigan State University. Readers used to sneak into MSU's Clarion archive to read this story they'd heard so much about.

Editors loved the story, but were afraid to publish it, even though they all agreed that it was great and memorable. To be honest, I'm not sure many editors would publish the story, even now.

In the years since this story first appeared, Nina has published over a dozen novels, won a Nebula award, and has been nominated for more awards than I can remember.

Much as I want to tell you more about "Savage Breasts," I won't. This one really can speak for itself.

Savage Breasts

Nina Kiriki Hoffman

I was only a lonely leftover on the table of Life. No one seemed interested in sampling me.

I was alone that day in the company cafeteria when I made the fateful decision which changed my life. If Gladys, the other secretary in my boss's office and my usual lunch companion, had been there, it might never have happened, but she had a dentist appointment. Alone with the day's entree, Spaghetti-O's, I sought company in a comic book I found on the table.

In the first blazing burst of inspiration I ever experienced, I cut out an ad on the back of the *Wonder Woman* comic book. "The Insult that Made a Woman Out of Wilma," it read. It showed a hipless, flat-chested girl being buried in the sand and abandoned by her date, who left her alone with the crabs as he followed a bosomy blonde off the page. Wilma eventually excavated herself, went home, kicked a chair, and sent away for Charlotte Atlas's pamphlet, "From Beanpole to Buxom in 20 days or your money back." Wilma read the pamphlet and developed breasts the size of breadboxes. She retrieved her boyfriend and rendered him acutely jealous by picking up a few hundred other men.

77

I emulated Wilma's example and sent away for the pamphlet and the equipment that came with it.

When my pamphlet and my powder-pink exerciser arrived, I felt a vague sense of unease. Some of the ink in the pamphlet was blurry. A few pages were repeated. Others were missing. Sensing that my uncharacteristic spurt of enthusiasm would dry up if I took the time to send for a replacement, I plunged into the exercises in the book (those I could decipher) and performed them faithfully for the requisite twenty days. My breasts blossomed. Men on the streets whistled. Guys at the office looked up when I jiggled past.

I felt like a palm tree hand-pollinated for the first time. I began to have clusters of dates. I was pawed, pleasured, and played with. I experienced lots of stuff I had only read about before, and I mostly loved it after the first few times. The desert I'd spent my life in vanished; everything I touched here in the center of the mirage seemed real, intense, throbbing with life. I exercised harder, hoping to make the reality realler.

Then parts of me began to fight back.

I reclined on Maxwell's couch, my hands behind my head, as he unbuttoned my shirt, unhooked my new, enormous, front-hook bra, and opened both wide. He kissed my stomach. He feathered kisses up my body. Suddenly my left breast flexed and punched him in the face. He was surprised. He looked at me suspiciously. I was surprised myself. I studied my left breast. It lay there gently bobbing like a Japanese glass float on a quiet sea. Innocent. Waiting.

Maxwell stared at my face. Then he shook his head. He eyed my breasts. Slowly he leaned closer. His lips drew back in a pucker. I waited, tingling, for them to flutter on my abdomen again. No such luck. Both breasts surged up and gave him a double whammy.

It took me an hour to wake him up. Once I got him conscious, he told me to get out! Out! And take my unnatural equipment with me. I collected my purse and coat and, with a last look at him as he lay there on the floor by the couch, I left.

In the elevator my breasts punched a man who was smoking a cigar. He coughed, choked, and called me unladylike. A woman told me I had done the right thing.

When I got home I took off my clothes and looked at myself in the mirror. What beautiful breasts. Pendulous. Centerfold quality. Heavy as water balloons. Firm as paperweights. I would be sorry to say goodbye to them. I sighed, and they bobbled. "Well, guys, no more exercise for you," I said. I would have to let them go. I couldn't let my breasts become a Menace to Mankind. I would rather be noble and suffer a bunch.

I took a shower and went to bed.

That night I had wild dreams. Something was chasing me, and I was chasing something else. I thought maybe I was chasing myself, and that scared me silly. I kept trying to wake up, but to no avail. When I finally woke, exhausted and sweaty, in the morning, I discovered my sheets twisted around my legs. My powder-pink exerciser lay beside me in the bed. My upper arms ached the way they did after a good workout.

At work, my breasts interfered with my typing. The minute I looked away from my typewriter keyboard to glance at my steno pad, my breasts pushed between my hands, monopolized the keys, and drove my Selectric to distraction. After an hour of trying to cope with this I told my boss I had a sick headache. He didn't want me to go home. "Mae June, you're quite an ornament to the office these days," he said. "Can't you just sit out there and look pretty and suffering? More and more of my clients have remarked on how you spruce up the decor. If that clackety-clacking bothers your pretty little head, why, I'll get Gladys to take your work and hers and type in the closet."

"Thank you, sir," I said. I went back out in the front room and sat far away from everything my breasts could knock over. Gladys sent me vicious looks as she flat-chestedly crouched over her early-model IBM and worked twice as hard as usual.

For a while I was happy just to rest. After all that nocturnal exertion, I was tired. My chair wasn't comfortable, but my body didn't care. Then I started feeling rotten. I watched Gladys. She had scruffy hair that kept falling out of its bobby pins and into her face. She kept her fingernails short and unpolished and she didn't seem to care how carelessly she chose her clothes. She reminded me of the way I had looked two months earlier, before men started getting interested in me and giving me advice on what to wear and what to do with my hair. Gladys and I no longer went to lunch together. These days I usually took the boss's clients to lunch.

"Why don't you tell the boss you have a sick headache too?" I asked. "There's nothing here that can't wait 'til tomorrow."

"He'd fire me, you fool. I can't waggle my femininity in his face like you can. Mae June, you're a cheater."

"I didn't mean to cheat," I said. "I can't help it." I looked at her face to see if she remembered how we used to talk at lunch. "Watch this, Gladys." I turned back to my typewriter and pulled off the cover. The instant I inserted paper, my breasts reached up and parked on the typewriter keys. I leaned back, straightening up, then tried to type the date in the upper right-hand corner of the page. Plomp plomp. No dice. I looked at Gladys. She had that kind of look that says *eyoo, ick, that's creepy, show it to me again.*

I opened my mouth to explain about Wilma's insult and Charlotte Atlas when my breasts firmed up. I found myself leaning back to display me at an advantage. One of the boss's clients had walked in.

"Mae June, my nymphlet," said this guy, Burl Weaver. I had been to lunch with him before. I kind of liked him.

Gladys touched the intercom. "Sir, Mr. Weaver is here."

"Aw, Gladys," said Burl, one of the few men who had learned her name as well as mine, "why'd you haveta spoil it? I didn't come here for business."

"Burl?" the boss asked over the intercom. "What does he want?"

Burl strode over to my desk and pushed my transmit button. "I'd like to borrow your secretary for the afternoon, Otis. Any objections?"

"Why no, Burl, none at all." Burl is one of our biggest accounts. We produce the plastic for the records his company produces. "Mae June, you be good to Burl now."

Burl pressed my transmit button for me. I leaned as near to my speaker as I could get. "Yes, sir," I said. With tons of trepidation, I rose to my feet. My previous acquaintance with Burl had gone further than my acquaintance with Maxwell yesterday. Now that my breasts were seceding from my body, how could I be sure I'd be nice to Burl? What if I lost the company our biggest account?

With my breasts thrust out before me like dogs hot on a scent, I followed Burl out of the office, giving Gladys a misery-laden glance as I closed the door behind me. She gave me a suffering nod in return. At least there was somebody on my side, I thought, as Burl and I got on the elevator. I tried to cross my arms over my breasts but they pushed my arms away. A familiar feeling of helplessness, one I knew well from before I sent away for that pamphlet, washed over me. Except this time I didn't feel my fate lay on the knees of the gods. No. My life was in the hands of my breasts, and they seemed determined to throw it away.

Burl waited until the elevator got midway between floors, then hit the stop button. "Just think, Mae June, here we are, suspended in midair," he said. "Think we can hump hard enough to make this thing drop? Wanna try? Think we'll even notice when she hits bottom?" With each sentence he got closer to me, until at last he was pulling the zip down the back of my dress.

I smiled at Burl and wondered what would happen next. I

felt like an interested spectator at a sports event. Burl pulled my dress down around my waist.

"You sure look nice today, Mae June, " he said, staring at my front, then at my lips. My breasts bobbled obligingly, and he looked down at them again. "Like you got little joy machines inside," he said, gently unhooking my bra.

Joy buzzers, I thought. Jolt city.

"You like me, don't you, Mae June? I can be real nice." He stroked me.

"Sure I like you, Burl."

"Would you like to work for me? I sure like you, Mae June. I'd like to put you in a nice little apartment on the top story of a real tall building with an elevator in it." As he talked, he kneaded at me like a kitten. "An express elevator. It would only stop at your floor and the basement. We could lock it from the inside. We could ride it. Up. Down. Up. Down. Hell, we could put a double bed in it. You'd like that, wouldn't you, Mae June?"

"Yes, Burl." When would my mammaries make their move?

He bent his head forward to pull down his own zipper, and they conked him. "Wha?" he said as he recoiled and collapsed gracefully to the floor. "How the heck did you do that, Mae June?"

I decided Burl had a harder head than Maxwell.

"Your hands are all snarled up in your dress. You been taking aikido or something?"

"No, Burl."

"Jeepers, if you didn't like me, you shoulda said something. I woulda left you alone."

"But I do like you, Burl. It's my breasts. They make their own decisions."

He lay on the floor and looked up at me. 'That's the dumbest-assed thing I ever heard," he said. He rolled over and got to his feet. Then he came over, leaned toward me, and glared at my breasts. The left one flexed. He jumped back just in time. "Mae June, are you possessed?"

"Yes!" That must be it. The devil was in my breasts. I wondered what I had done to deserve such a fate. I wasn't even religious.

Burl made the sign of the cross over my breasts. Nothing happened. "That's not it," he said. "Maybe it's your subconscious. You hate men. Something like that. So how come this didn't happen last time, huh?" He began pacing.

"They were waiting to get strong enough. Oh, Burl, what am I going to do?"

"Get dressed. I think you better see a doctor, Mae June. Maybe we can get 'em tranquilized or something. I don't like the way they're sitting there, watching me."

I managed to hook my bra without too much trouble. Burl zipped me up and turned the elevator operational again. "Do you hate me?" I asked him on the way down.

"Course I don't hate you," he said, shifting a step away from me. "You're real pretty, Mae June. Just as soon as you get yourself under control, you're gonna make somebody a real nice little something. I just don't want to take too many chances. Suppose what you've got is contagious? Suppose some of my body parts decide they don't like women? Let's be rational about this, huh?"

"I mean—you won't drop the contract with IPP, will you?"

"Shoot no. You worried about job security? I like that in a woman. You got sense. I won't complain. But I hope you got Blue Cross. You may have to get those knockers psychoanalyzed or something."

He offered to drive me to a doctor or the hospital. I told him I'd take the bus. He tried to get me to change my mind. He failed. I watched him drive away. Then I went home.

I picked up the powder-pink exerciser and took it to the window. My apartment was on the tenth floor. I was just going to drop the exerciser out the window when I looked down and saw Gladys's red coat wrapped around Gladys. My doorbell rang. I buzzed her into the building.

By the time she arrived at my front door I had collapsed on the couch, still holding the exerciser. "It's open," I called when she knocked. My arms were pumping the exerciser as I lay there. I thought about trying to stop exercising, but decided it was too much effort. "How'd you know I'd be home?" I asked Gladys as she came in and took off her coat.

"Burl stopped by the office."

"Did he say what happened?"

"No. He said he was worried about you. What did happen?"

They punched him." I pumped the exerciser harder. "What am I going to do? I can't type, and now I can't even do lunch." I glared at my breasts. "You want us to starve?"

They were doing push-ups and didn't answer.

Gladys sat on a chair across from me and leaned forward, her gaze fixed on my new features. Her mouth was open.

My arms stopped pumping without me having anything to say about it. My left arm handed the exerciser to her. Her gaze still locked on my breasts, Gladys gripped the powder-pink exerciser and went to work.

"Don't," I said, sitting up. Startled, she fell against the chair back. "Do you want this to happen to you?"

"I—I—" She gulped and dropped the exerciser.

"I don't know what they want!" I stared at them with loathing. "It won't be long before the boss realizes I'm not an asset. Then what am I going to do?"

"You...you have a lot of career choices," said Gladys. "Like —have you ever considered mud wrestling?"

"What?"

"Exotic dancing?" She blinked. She licked her upper lip. "You could join the FBI, I bet. 'My breasts punched out spies for God and country.' You could sell your story to the *Enquirer*. 'Double-breasted Death.' Sounds like a slick detective movie from the Thirties. You could—"

"Stop," I said, "I don't want to hear any more."

"I'm sorry," she said after a minute. She got up and made tea.

We were sitting there sipping it when she had another brainstorm. "What do they want? You've been asking that yourself. What are breasts for, anyway?"

"Sex and babies," I said.

We looked at each other. We looked away. All those lunches, and we had never talked about it. I bet she only knew what she read in books too.

She stared at the braided rug on the floor. "Were you...protected?"

I stared at the floor too. "I don't think so."

"They have tests you can do at home."

I thought it was Burl's, so my breasts and I went to visit him. "You talk to them," I said. "If they think you're the father, maybe they won't beat you up anymore. Maybe they're just fending off all other comers."

Between the three of them they reached an arrangement. I moved into that penthouse apartment.

I shudder to think what they'll do when the baby comes.

Bits and Pieces

LISA TUTTLE

Introduction

A few years ago, a regional advertising organization did a series of ads in which people would find bits of flesh lying around places, such as the beach. It was to encourage people to lose weight, which I found a little creepy, primarily because those ads reminded me strongly of this story.

Lisa Tuttle's first novel, Windhaven, *which she co-wrote with George R.R. Martin, appeared in 1981. She's been publishing steadily ever since, publishing more than a dozen novels under her own name, and several more under pen names. She's also edited many volumes, and wrote a lot of nonfiction, including* The Encyclopedia of Feminism.

Lisa's award-winning short fiction always combines metaphor with strong storytelling, and in that, this story fits right into the rest of her work.

Bits and Pieces

Lisa Tuttle

On the morning after Ralph left her Fay found a foot in her bed.

It was Ralph's foot, but how could he have left it behind? What did it mean? She sat on the edge of the bed holding it in her hand, examining it. It was a long, pale, narrow, rather elegant foot. At the top, where you would expect it to grow into an ankle, the foot ended in a slight, skin-covered concavity. There was no sign of blood or severed flesh or bone or scar tissue, nor were there any corns or bunions, over-long nails or dirt. Ralph was a man who looked after his feet.

Lying there in her hand it felt as alive as a motionless foot ever feels; impossible as it seemed, she believed it was real. Ralph wasn't a practical joker, and yet—a foot wasn't something you left behind without noticing. She wondered how he was managing to get around on just one foot. Was it a message? Some obscure consolation for her feeling that, losing him, she had lost a piece of herself?

He had made it clear he no longer wanted to be involved with her. His goodbye had sounded final. But maybe he would get in touch when he realized she still had something of his. Although she knew she ought to be trying to forget him, she felt oddly grateful for this unexpected gift. She wrapped the foot in a silk scarf and put it in the dresser's bottom drawer, to keep for him.

Two days later, tidying the bedroom, she found his other foot under the bed. She had to check the drawer to make sure it wasn't the same one, gone wandering. But it was still there, one right foot, and she was holding the left one. She wrapped the two of them together in the white silk scarf and put them away.

Time passed and Ralph did not get in touch. Fay knew from friends that he was still around, and as she never heard any suggestion that he was now crippled, she began to wonder if the feet had been some sort of hallucination. She kept meaning to look in the bottom drawer, but somehow she kept forgetting.

The relationship with Ralph, while it lasted, had been a serious, deeply meaningful one for them both, she thought; she knew from the start there was no hope of that with Freddy. Fay was a responsible person who believed the act of sex should be accompanied by love and a certain degree of commitment; she detested the very idea of "casual sex"—but she'd been six months without a man in her bed, and Freddy was irresistible.

He was warm and cuddly and friendly, the perfect teddy bear. Within minutes of meeting him she was thinking about sleeping with him—although it was the comfort and coziness of bed he brought to mind rather than passion. As passive as a teddy bear, he would let himself be pursued. She met him with friends in a pub, and he offered to walk her home. Outside her door he hugged her. There was no kissing or groping; he just wrapped her in a warm, friendly embrace, where she clung to him longer and tighter than friendship required.

"Mmmm," he said, appreciatively, smiling down at her, his eyes button-bright, "I could do this all night."

"What a good idea," she said.

After they had made love she decided he was less a teddy bear than a cat. Like a cat in the sensual way he moved and rubbed his body against hers and responded to her touch: she could almost hear him purr. Other cat-like qualities, apparent after she had known him a little longer, were less appealing. Like a cat he was self-centered, basically lazy, and although she continued to enjoy him in bed, she did wish sometimes he would pay more attention to her pleasure instead of assuming that his was enough for them both. He seemed to expect her to be pleased no matter what time he turned up for dinner, even if he fell asleep in front of the fire immediately after. And, like many cats, he had more than one home.

Finding out about his other home—hearing that other woman's tear-clogged voice down the phone—decided her to end it. It wasn't—or so she told him—that she wanted to have him all to herself. But she wouldn't be responsible for another woman's sorrow.

He understood her feelings. He was wrong, and she was right. He was remorseful, apologetic, and quite incapable of changing. But he would miss her very much. He gave her a friendly hug before they parted, but once they started hugging it was hard to stop, and they tumbled into bed again.

That had to be the last time. She knew she could be firmer with him on the phone than in person, so she told him he was not to visit unless she first invited him. Sadly, he agreed.

And that was that. Going back into the bedroom she saw the duvet rucked up as if there was someone still in the bed. It made her shiver. If she hadn't just seen him out the door, and closed it behind him she might have thought...Determined to put an end to such mournful nonsense she flung the duvet aside, and there he was.

Well, part of him.

Lying on the bed was a headless, neckless, armless, legless torso. Or at least the back side of one. As with Ralph's feet there was nothing unpleasant about it, no blood or gaping wounds. If you could ignore the sheer impossibility of it, there was nothing wrong with Freddy's back at all. It looked just like the body she had been embracing a few minutes before, and felt...

Tentatively, she reached out and touched it. It was warm and smooth, with the firm, elastic give of live flesh. She could not resist stroking it the way she knew he liked, teasing with her nails to make the skin prickle into goose bumps, running her fingers all the way from the top of the spine to the base, and over the curve of the buttocks where the body ended.

She drew her hand back, shocked. What was this? It seemed so much like Freddy, but how could it be when she had seen him, minutes before, walking out the door, fully equipped with all his body parts? Was it possible that there was nothing, now, but air filling out his jumper and jeans?

She sat down, took hold of the torso where the shoulders ended in smooth, fleshy hollows, and heaved it over. The chest was as she remembered, babyishly pink nipples peeking out of a scumble of ginger hair, but below the flat stomach only more flatness. His genitals were missing, as utterly and completely gone as if they had never been thought of. Her stomach twisted with shock and horror although, a moment later, she had to ask herself why that particular lack should matter so much more than the absence of his head—which she had accepted remarkably calmly. After all, this wasn't the real Freddy, only some sort of partial memory of his body inexplicably made flesh.

She went over to the dresser and crouched before the bottom drawer. Yes, they were still there. They didn't appear to have decayed or faded or changed in any way. Letting the silk scarf fall away she gazed at the naked feet and realized that she felt differently about Ralph. She had been unhappy when he left, but she had also been, without admitting it even to herself, furiously angry with him. And the anger had passed. The bitterness was gone, and she felt only affection now as she caressed his feet and remembered the good times. Eventually, with a sigh that mingled fondness and regret, she wrapped them up and put them away. Then she returned to her current problem: what to do with the part Freddy had left behind.

For a moment she thought of leaving it in the bed. He'd

always been *so* nice to sleep with…But no. She had to finish what she had begun; she couldn't continue sleeping with part of Freddy all the time when all of Freddy part of the time had not been enough for her. She would never be able to get on with her life, she would never dare bring anyone new home with her.

It would have to go in the wardrobe. The only other option was the hall closet which was cold and smelled slightly of damp. So, wrapping it in her best silken dressing gown, securing it with a tie around the waist, she stored Freddy's torso in the wardrobe behind her clothes.

Freddy phoned the next week. He didn't mention missing anything but her, and she almost told him about finding his torso in her bed. But how could she? If she told him, he'd insist on coming over to see it, and if he came over she'd be back to having an affair with him. That wasn't what she was after, was it? She hesitated, and then asked if he was still living with Matilda.

"Oh, more or less," he said. "Yes."

So she didn't tell him. She tried to forget him, and hoped to meet someone else, someone who would occupy the man-sized empty space in her life.

Meanwhile, Freddy continued to phone her once a week— friendly calls, because he wanted to stay friends. After a while she realized, from comments he let drop, that he was seeing another woman; that once again he had two homes. As always, she resisted the temptation she felt to invite him over, but she felt wretchedly lonely that evening.

For the first time since she had stored it away, she took out his body. Trembling a little, ashamed of herself, she took it to bed. She so wanted someone to hold. The body felt just like Freddy, warm and solid and smooth in the same way; it even smelled like him, although now with a faint overlay of her own perfume from her clothes. She held it for a while, but the lack of arms and head was too peculiar. She found that if she lay with her back against his and tucked her legs up so she couldn't feel his missing legs, it was almost like being in bed with Freddy.

She slept well that night, better than she had for weeks. "My teddy bear," she murmured as she packed him away again in the morning. It was like having a secret weapon. The comfort of a warm body in bed with her at night relaxed her, and made her more self-confident. She no longer felt any need to invite Freddy over, and when he called it was easy to talk to him without getting more involved, as if they'd always been just friends. And now that she wasn't looking, there seemed to be more men around.

One of them, Paul, who worked for the same company in a different department, asked her out. Lately she had kept running into him, and he seemed to have a lot of business which took him to her part of the building, but it didn't register on her that this was no coincidence until he asked if she was doing anything that Saturday night. After that, his interest in her seemed so obvious that she couldn't imagine why she hadn't noticed earlier.

The most likely reason she hadn't noticed was that she didn't care. She felt instinctively that he wasn't her type; they had little in common. But his unexpected interest flattered her, and made him seem more attractive, and so she agreed to go out with him.

It was a mistake, she thought, uneasily, when Saturday night came around and Paul took her to a very expensive restaurant. He was not unintelligent, certainly not bad-looking, but there was something a little too glossy and humorless about him. He was interested in money, and cars, and computers—and her. He dressed well, and he knew the right things to say, but she imagined he had learned them out of a book. He was awfully single-minded, and seemed intent on seduction, which made her nervous, and she spent too much of the evening trying to think of some way of getting out of inviting him in for coffee when he took her home. It was no good; when the time came, he invited himself in.

She knew it wasn't fair to make comparisons, but Paul was the complete opposite of Freddy. Where Freddy sat back and waited calmly to be stroked, Paul kept edging closer, trying to crawl into her lap. And his hands were everywhere. From the very start of the evening he had stood and walked too close to her, and she didn't like the way he had of touching her, as if casually making a point, staking a physical claim to her.

For the next hour she fended him off. It was a wordless battle which neither of them would admit to. When he left, she lacked the energy to refuse a return match, the following weekend.

They went to the theater, and afterward to his place—he said he wanted to show her his computer. She expected another battle, but he was a perfect gentleman. Feeling safer, she agreed to a third date, and then drank too much; the drink loosened her inhibitions, she was too tired to resist his persistent pressure, and finally took him into her bed.

The sex was not entirely a success—for her, anyway—but it would doubtless get better as they got to know each other, she thought, and she was just allowing herself a few modest fantasies about the future, concentrating on the things she thought she liked about him, when he said he had to go.

The man who had been hotly all over her was suddenly distant and cool, almost rude in his haste to leave. She tried to find excuses for him, but when he had gone, and she discovered his hands were still in her bed, she knew he did not mean to return.

The hands were nestling beneath a pillow like a couple of soft-shelled crabs. She shuddered at the sight of them; shouted and threw her shoes at them. The left hand twitched when struck, but otherwise they didn't move.

How dare he leave his hands! She didn't want anything to remember him by! She certainly hadn't been in love with him.

Fay looked around for something else to throw, and then felt ashamed of herself. Paul was a creep, but it wasn't fair to take it out on his hands. They hadn't hurt her; they had done their best to give her pleasure—they might have succeeded if she'd liked their owner more.

But she didn't like their owner—she had to admit she wasn't really sorry he wouldn't be back—so why was she stuck with his hands? She could hardly give them back. She could already guess how he would avoid her at work, and she wasn't about to add to his inflated ego by pursuing him. But it didn't seem possible to throw them out, either.

She found a shoebox to put them in—she didn't bother about wrapping them—and then put the box away out of sight on the highest shelf of the kitchen cupboard, among the cracked plates, odd saucers, and empty jars which she'd kept because they might someday be useful.

The hands made her think a little differently about what had happened. She had been in love with Ralph and also, for all her attempts to rationalize her feelings, with Freddy—she hadn't wanted either of them to go. It made a kind of sense for her to fantasize that they'd left bits of themselves behind, but that didn't apply to her feelings for Paul. She absolutely refused to believe that her subconscious was responsible for the hands in the kitchen cupboard.

So if not her subconscious, then what? Was it the bed? She stood in the bedroom and looked at it, trying to perceive some sorcery in the brand-name mattress or the pine frame. She had bought the bed for Ralph, really; he had complained so about the futon she had when they met, declaring that it was not only too short, but also bad for his back. He had told her that pine beds were good and also cheap, and although she didn't agree with his assessment of the price, she had bought one. It was the most expensive thing she owned. Was it also haunted?

She could test it; invite friends to stay…Would any man who made love in this bed leave a part of himself behind, or only those who made love to her? Only for the last time? But how did it know? How could it, before she herself knew a relationship was over? What if she lured Paul back—would some other body part appear when he left? Or would the hands disappear?

Once she had thought of this, she knew she had to find out. She tried to forget the idea but could not. Days passed, and Paul did not get in touch—he avoided her at work, as she had guessed he would—and she told herself to let him go. Good riddance. To pursue him would be humiliating. It wasn't even as if she were in love with him, after all.

She told herself not to be a fool, but chance and business kept taking her to his part of the building. When forced to acknowledge her his voice was polite and he did not stand too close; he spoke as if they'd never met outside working hours; as if he'd never really noticed her as a woman. She saw him, an hour later, leaning confidentially over one of the newer secretaries, his hand touching her hip.

She felt a stab of jealous frustration. No wonder she couldn't attract his attention; he had already moved on to fresh prey.

Another week went by, but she would not accept defeat. She phoned him up and invited him to dinner. He said his weekends were awfully busy just now. She suggested a weeknight. He hesitated—surprised by her persistence? Contemptuous? Flattered? —and then said he was involved with someone, actually. Despising herself, Fay said lightly that of course she understood. She said that in fact, she herself was involved in a long-standing relationship, but her fellow had been abroad for the past few months, and she got bored and lonely in the evenings. She'd enjoyed herself so much with Paul that she had hoped they'd be able to get together again sometime; that was all.

That changed the temperature. He said he was afraid he couldn't manage dinner, but if she liked, he could drop by later one evening—maybe tomorrow, around ten?

He was on her as soon as he was through the door. She tried to fend him off with offers of drink, but he didn't seem to hear. His hands were everywhere, grabbing, fondling, probing, as undeniably real as they'd ever been.

"Wait, wait," she said, laughing but not amused. "Can't we…talk?"

He paused, holding her around the waist, and looked down at her. He was bigger than she remembered. "We could have talked on the phone."

"I know, but…"

"Is there something we need to talk about?"

"Well, no, nothing specific, but…"

"Did you invite me over here to talk? Did I misunderstand?"

"No."

"All right." His mouth came down, wet and devouring, on hers, and she gave in.

But not on the couch, she thought, a few minutes later. "Bed," she gasped, breaking away. "In the bedroom."

"Good idea."

But it no longer seemed like a good idea to her. As she watched him strip off his clothes she thought this was probably the worst idea she'd ever had. She didn't want him in her bed again; she didn't want sex with him. How could she have thought, for even a minute, that she could have sex for such a cold-blooded, ulterior motive?

"I thought you were in a hurry," he said. "Get your clothes off." Naked, he reached for her.

She backed away. "I'm sorry, I shouldn't have called you, I'm sorry—"

"Don't apologize. It's very sexy when a woman knows what she wants and asks for it." He'd unbuttoned her blouse and unhooked her bra earlier, and now tried to remove them. She tried to stop him, and he pinioned her wrists.

"This is a mistake, I don't want this, you have to go."

"Like hell."

"I'm sorry, Paul, but I mean it."

He smiled humorlessly. "You mean you want me to force you."

"No!"

He pushed her down on the bed, got her skirt off despite her struggles, then ripped her tights.

"Stop it!"

"I wouldn't have thought you liked this sort of thing," he mused.

"I don't, I'm telling the truth, I don't want to have sex, I want you to leave." Her voice wobbled all over the place. "Look, I'm sorry, I'm really sorry, but I can't, not now." Tears leaked out of her eyes. "Please. You don't understand. This isn't a game." She was completely naked now and he was naked on top of her.

"This *is* a game," he said calmly. "And I do understand. You've been chasing me for weeks. I know what you want. A minute ago, you were begging me to take you to bed. Now you're embarrassed. You want me to force you. I don't want to force you, but if I have to, I will."

"No."

"It's up to you," he said. "You can give, or I can take. That simple."

She had never thought rape could be that simple. She bit one of the arms that held her down. He slapped her hard.

"I told you," he said. "You can give, or I can take. It's that simple. It's your choice."

Frightened by his strength, seeing no choice at all, she gave in.

Afterward, she was not surprised when she discovered what he had left in her bed. What else should it be? It was just what she deserved.

It was ugly, yet there was something oddly appealing in the sight of it nestling in a fold of the duvet; she was reminded of her teenage passion for collecting bean-bag creatures. She used to line them up across her bed. This could have been one of them: maybe a squashy elephant's head with a fat nose. She went on staring at it for a long time, lying on her side on the bed, emotionally numbed and physically exhausted, unable either to get up or to go to sleep. She told herself she should get rid of it, that she could take her aggressions out on it, cut it up, at least throw it, and the pair of hands, out with the rest of her unwanted garbage. But it was hard to connect this bean-bag creature with Paul and what he had done to her. She realized she had scarcely more than glimpsed his genitals; no wonder she couldn't believe this floppy creature could have had anything to do with her rape. The longer she looked at it, the less she could believe it was that horrible man's. It, too, had been abused by him. And it wasn't his now, it was hers. OK, Paul had been the catalyst, somehow, but this set of genitalia had been born from the bed and her own desire; it was an entirely new thing.

Eventually she fell asleep, still gazing at it. When she opened her eyes in the morning it was like seeing an old friend. She wouldn't get rid of it. She put it in a pillowcase and stashed the parcel among the scarves, shawls and sweaters on the shelf at the top of the wardrobe.

She decided to put the past behind her. She didn't think about Paul or Ralph or even Freddy. Although most nights she slept with Freddy's body, that was a decision made on the same basis, and with no more emotion, as whether she slept with the duvet or the electric blanket. Freddy's body wasn't Freddy's anymore; it was hers.

The only men in her life now were friends. She wasn't looking for romance, and she seldom thought about sex. If she wanted male companionship there was Christopher, a platonic friend from school, or Marcus, her next-door neighbor, or Freddy. They still talked on the phone frequently, and very occasionally met in town for a drink or a meal, but she had never invited him over since their break-up, so it was a shock one evening to answer the door and discover him standing outside.

He looked sheepish. "I'm sorry," he said. "I know I should have called first, but I couldn't find a working phone, and...I hope you don't mind. I need somebody to talk to. Matilda's thrown me out."

And not only Matilda, but also the latest other woman. He poured out his woes, and she made dinner, and they drank wine and talked for hours.

"Do you have somewhere to stay?" she asked at last.

"I could go to my sister's. I stay there a lot anyway. She's got a spare room—I've even got my own key. But—" He gave her his old look, desirous but undemanding. "Actually, Fay, I was hoping I could stay with you tonight."

She discovered he was still irresistible.

Her last thought before she fell asleep was how strange it was to sleep with someone who had arms and legs.

In the morning she woke enough to feel him kiss her, but she didn't realize it was a kiss goodbye, for she could still feel his legs entwined with her own.

But the rest of him was gone, and probably for good this time, she discovered when she woke up completely. For a man with such a smooth-skinned body he had extremely hairy legs, she thought, sitting on the bed and staring at the unattached limbs. And for a woman who had just been used and left again, she felt awfully cheerful.

She got Ralph's feet out of the drawer—thinking how much thinner and more elegant they were than Freddy's—and, giggling to herself, pressed the right foot to the bottom of the right leg, just to see how it looked.

It looked as if it was growing there and always had been. When she tried to pull it away, it wouldn't come. She couldn't even see a join. Anyone else might have thought it was perfectly natural; it probably only looked odd to her because she knew it wasn't. When she did the same thing with the left foot and left leg, the same thing happened.

So then, feeling daring, she took Freddy's torso out of the wardrobe and laid it down on the bed just above the legs. She pushed the legs up close, so they looked as if they were growing out of the torso—and then they were. She sat it up, finding that it was as flexible and responsive as a real, live person, not at all a dead weight, and she sat on the edge of the bed beside it and looked down at its empty lap.

"Don't go away; I have just the thing for Sir," she said.

The genitals were really the wrong size and skin-tone for Freddy's long, pale body, but they nestled gratefully into his crotch, obviously happy in their new home.

The body was happy, too. There was new life in it—not Freddy's, not Paul's, not Ralph's, but a new being created out of their old parts. She wasn't imagining it. Not propped up, it was sitting beside her, holding itself up, alert and waiting. When she leaned closer she could feel a heart beating within the chest, sending the blood coursing through a network of veins and arteries. She reached out to stroke the little elephant-head slumbering between the legs, and as she touched it, it stirred and sat up.

She was sexually excited, too, and, at the same time, horrified. There had to be something wrong with her to want to have sex with this incomplete collection of body parts. All right, it wasn't dead, so at least what she felt wasn't necrophilia, but what was it? A man without arms was merely disabled, but was a man without a head a man at all? Whatever had happened to her belief in the importance of relationships? They couldn't even communicate, except by touch, and then only at her initiative. All he could do was respond to her will. She thought of Paul's hands, how she had been groped, forced, slapped, and held down by them, and was just as glad they remained unattached, safely removed to the kitchen cupboard. Safe sex, she thought, and giggled. In response to the vibration, the body listed a little in her direction.

She got off the bed and moved away, then stood and watched it swaying indecisively. She felt a little sorry for it, being so utterly dependent on her, and that cooled her ardor. It wasn't right, she couldn't use it as a kind of live sex-aid—not as it was. She was going to have to find it a head, or forget about it.

She wrapped the body in a sheet to keep the dust off and

stored it under the bed. She couldn't sleep with it anymore. In its headless state it was too disturbing. "Don't worry," she said, although it couldn't hear her. "This isn't forever."

She started her head-hunt. She knew it might take some time, but she was going to be careful; she didn't want another bad experience. It wouldn't be worth it. Something good had come out of the Paul experience, but heads—or faces, anyway —were so much harder to depersonalize. If it looked like Freddy or Paul in the face, she knew she would respond to it as Freddy or Paul, and what was the point of that? She wanted to find someone new, someone she didn't know, but also someone she liked; someone she could find attractive, go to bed with, and be parted from without the traumas of love or hate.

She hoped it wasn't an impossible paradox.

She asked friends for introductions, she signed up for classes, joined clubs, went to parties, talked to men in supermarkets and on buses, answered personal ads. And then Marcus dropped by one evening, and asked if she wanted to go to a movie with him.

They had seen a lot of movies and shared a fair number of pizzas over the past two years, but although she liked him, she knew very little about him. She didn't even know for sure that he was heterosexual. She occasionally saw him with other women, but the relationships seemed to be platonic. Because he was younger than she was, delicate-looking and with a penchant for what she thought of as "arty" clothes, because he didn't talk about sex and had never touched her, the idea of having sex with him had never crossed her mind. Now, seeing his clean-shaven, rather pretty face as if for the first time, it did.

"What a good idea," she said.

After the movie, after the pizza and a lot of wine, after he'd said he probably should be going, Fay put her hand on his leg and suggested he stay. He seemed keen enough—if surprised— but after she got him into bed he quickly lost his erection and nothing either of them did made any difference.

"It's not your fault," he said anxiously. It had not occurred to her that it could be. "Oh, God, this is awful," he went on. "If you only knew how I've dreamed of this...Only I never thought, never dared to hope, that you could want me too, and now... you're so wonderful, and kind, and beautiful, and you deserve so much, and you must think I'm completely useless."

"I think it's probably the wine," she said. "We both had too much to drink. Maybe you should go on home...I think we'd both sleep better in our own beds, alone."

"Oh, God, you don't hate me, do you? You will give me another chance, won't you, Fay? Please?"

"Don't worry about it. Yes, Marcus, yes, of course I will. Now, good night."

She found nothing in her bed afterward; she hadn't expected to. But neither did she expect the flowers that arrived the next day, and the day after that.

He took her out to dinner on Friday night—not pizza this time—and afterward, in her house, in her bed, they did what they had come together to do. She fell asleep, supremely satisfied, in his arms. In the morning he was eager to make love again, and Fay might have been interested—he had proved himself to be a very tender and skilful lover—but she was too impatient. She had only wanted him for one thing, and the sooner he left her, the sooner she would get it.

"I think you'd better go, Marcus. Let's not drag this out," she said.

"What do you mean?"

"I mean this was a mistake, we shouldn't have made love, we're really just friends who had too much to drink, so..."

He looked pale, even against the pale linen. "But I love you."

There was a time when such a statement, in such circumstances, would have made her happy, but the Fay who had loved, and expected to be loved in return, by the men she took to bed, seemed like another person now.

"But I don't love you."

"Then why did you—"

"Look, I don't want to argue. I don't want to say something that might hurt you. I want us to be friends, that's all, the way we used to be." She got up, since he still hadn't moved, and put on her robe.

"Are you saying you never want to see me again?"

She looked down at him. He really did have a nice face, and the pain that was on it now—that she had put there—made her look away hastily in shame. "Of course I do. You've been a good neighbor and a good friend. I hope we can go on being that. Only…" She tried to remember what someone had said to her once, was it Ralph? "Only I can't be what you want me to be. I still care about you, of course. But I don't love you in that way. So we'd better part. You'll see it's for the best, in time. You'll find someone else."

"You mean you will."

Startled, she looked back at him. Wasn't that what she had said to Ralph? She couldn't think how to answer him. But Marcus was out of bed, getting dressed, and didn't seem to expect an answer.

"I'll go," he said. "Because you ask me to. But I meant what I said. I love you. You know where I live. If you want me…if you change your mind…"

"Yes, of course. Goodbye, Marcus, I'm sorry."

She walked him to the door, saw him out, and locked the door behind him. Now! She scurried back to the bedroom, but halted in the doorway as she had a sudden, nasty thought. What if it hadn't worked? What if, instead of a pretty face, she found, say, another pair of feet in her bed?

Then I'll do it again, she decided, and again and again until I get my man.

She stepped forward, grasped the edge of the duvet, and threw it aside with a conjurer's flourish.

There was nothing on the bare expanse of pale blue sheet; nothing but a few stray pubic hairs.

She picked up the pillows, each in turn, and shook them. She shook out the duvet, unfastening the cover to make sure there was nothing inside. She peered beneath the bed and poked around the sheet-wrapped body, even pulled the bed away from the wall, in case something had caught behind the headboard. Finally she crawled across the bed on her belly, nose to the sheet, examining every inch.

Nothing. He had left nothing.

But why? How?

They left parts because they weren't willing to give all. The bed preserved bits and pieces of men who wanted only pieces of her time, pieces of her body, for which they could pay only with pieces of their own.

Marcus wanted more than that. He wanted, and offered, everything. But she had refused him, so now she had nothing.

No, not nothing. She crouched down and pulled the sheet-wrapped form from beneath the bed, unwrapped it and reassured herself that the headless, armless body was still warm, still alive, still male, still hers. She felt the comforting stir of sexual desire in her own body as she aroused it in his, and she vowed she would not be defeated.

It would take thought and careful planning, but surely she could make one more lover leave her?

She spent the morning making preparations, and at about lunchtime she phoned Marcus and asked him to come over that evening.

"Did you really mean it when you said you loved me?"

"Yes."

"Because I want to ask you to do something for me, and I don't think you will."

"Fay, anything, what is it?"

"I'll have to tell you in person."

"I'll come over now."

She fell into his arms when he came in, and kissed him passionately. She felt his body respond, and when she looked at his face she saw the hurt had gone and a wondering joy replaced it.

"Let's go in the bedroom," she said. "I'm going to tell you everything; I'm going to tell you the truth about what I want, and you won't like it, I know."

"How can you know? How can you possibly know?" He stroked her back, smiling at her.

"Because it's not normal. It's a sexual thing."

"Try me."

They were in the bedroom now. She drew a deep breath. "Can I tie you to the bed?"

"Well." He laughed a little. "I've never done that before, but I don't see anything wrong with it. If it makes you happy."

"Can I do it?"

"Yes, why not."

"Now, I mean." Shielding the bedside cabinet with her body, she pulled out the ropes she had put there earlier. "Lie down."

He did as she said. "You don't want me to undress first?"

She shook her head, busily tying him to the bedposts.

"And what do I do now?" He strained upwards against the ropes, demonstrating how little he was capable of doing.

"Now you give me your head."

"What?"

"Other men have given me other parts; I want your head."

It was obvious he didn't know what she meant. She tried to remember how she had planned to explain; what, exactly, she wanted him to do. Should she show him the body under the bed? Would he understand then?

"Your head," she said again, and then she remembered the words. "It's simple. You can give it to me, or I can take it. It's your choice."

He still stared at her as if it wasn't simple at all. She got the knife out of the bedside cabinet, and held it so he could see. "You give, or I take. It's your choice."

Willie of the Jungle

STEVE PERRY

Introduction

One of my favorite Pulphouse *stories of all time is "Willie of the Jungle." After reading* Pulphouse, *Steve sent us some of what he calls his "wild hair" stories, stories he had to write, even though he knew there was no market for them.*

Years later, he mused to me that these stories were no longer wild hair stories because he knew that Pulphouse *(both the Hardback Magazine and the Fiction Magazine that Dean now edits) will strongly consider every such story that he writes.*

Steve had mostly given up on short stories in the early 1990s. He was busy with a TV career, a novel career, and a career in comics. He would throw off stories like this one, mostly to get them out of his head.

I'm glad he did so. Or else we might not have gotten to know Willie, who—believe me—you'll never forget.

Willie of the Jungle

Steve Perry

Bits and pieces, that's all Willie had, scattered chunks, half-seen fragments, but there was something he was supposed to do. Some place he was supposed to get to. Somehow. What? Where? How? Well. That was another game, Willie didn't have those rules: what he had was weird flashes coming out of nowhere once in a while. Confusing as hell, but there was something. What was it?

Willie shrugged and leaned his pale naked body against the paler bark of the fat alder tree. Being Lord of the Jungle had its problems sometimes.

He was forty feet above the spongy green mat of the rainforest's floor and he looked down upon sprawling, crawly thick ferns, young Douglas fir and hemlock and the decayed guck of a thousand moldy years—the last busily and damply smoldering its way to valuable petroleum tar. So far, the guck had only rotted as far as green-brown humus, weren't any dead dinosaurs to help it along this time. Young pre-oil down there had a ways to go, it did, maybe another fifty million years and a climate change or three, whatever.

Now how did he know that? And—was it important?

Willie leaned against the rough bark. Nah. Worry about it later—

Hello? Looky down there, Willie.

Willie looked. Tree cutters! Oh, ho.

Willie became one with the forest, he steeled himself into a statue that was as much tree as any branch, but he figured the two white men probably wouldn't see him up here if he jumped up and down and waved like crazy. White men in the forest were generally blind, pretty much deaf and for sure stupid, as he remembered. He thought he remembered. They sure couldn't smell him, likely they couldn't smell a tub full of snake shit over the stink of their gasoline-powered chain saws. White men. Gah.

Willie had a vagrant thought, something about white men, something he could not quite get his mind around....

Well. It didn't matter. What *mattered* were the two cutters down there, white men with their mechanical beavers, come fucking around in *Willie's* forest. Scaring his rabbits and trees and bears. Big men, dressed in short-legged and loose pants held up by wide suspenders, caulk boots with spikes that dug into the soft ground, bright plaid shirts and baseball caps that said Perennial Rye Grass and Caterpillar. Lumber jack-offs, come to slay Willie's trees.

Willie smiled. *That* would be the day.

The men passed directly under Willie's perch. Blindly, deafly, and stupidly. They stomped along, human tanks, shoving saplings aside, tromping mushrooms, crushing delicate ferns under their heavy boots. Ecological nitwits, both of them. Christ.

Willie let them pass. Only when the two men were a hundred yards away, hidden by heavy, old growth timber, did Willie come down. Down, and the wind rushed past him as he dropped the last five feet, sank into the springy ground and felt the cushion of the thick, moist humus under his bare feet. Right. That was how it went.

He raised from the crouch, stood tall in his rugged manhood, put his hands along the sides of his mouth, and took a deep breath. Then he did the yell: "Uhhhh-ahuhahuh-ah-uh-ahuhah-uh!"

It was a sort of sing-song yodel, but it was loud in the quiet woods, a chilling, gooseflesh producing cry. It always impressed the hell out of the rabbits and trees and bears, Willie knew, just as he knew it would also scare the living shit out of the white men.

Of course, almost everything scared the shit out of white men.

As a rule.

Willie bent and picked up his stick. The stick was an arm-long, arm-thick chunk of slightly curved hardwood. The cutters had walked right past it, blindly-deafly-and-stupidly, no surprise there. Willie hefted the heavy wood, got a good grip on it and said, "What say, stick, you want to take a little trip?"

The stick allowed as how it wouldn't mind, so Willie thought.

You could never be too sure with sticks.

Willie started running. He couldn't see them and they couldn't see him, but in a few seconds he would be right on top of the two cutters.

He ran lightly, one with his forest, his blood rumbling in his ears, his breath singing hah-hah-hah-hah in tune with his quick steps. He dodged his way through a thick stand of fifty-year-old almost-ripe evergreens and came smack into the little clearing where the two cutters stood nailed stock-still, listening for the yell again.

Even blind, deaf and stupid, they couldn't miss him now. They saw Willie. Finally.

"Motherfucker!" one of them said. "Gawd-damn!" the other one said.

Regular pair of Anglo-Saxon geniuses, these two.

The first cutter, that was Motherfucker, dropped his heavy

chain saw and turned to run. Willie read the man's mind by the way his legs pumped. Feet, do your stuff!

Willie was on him before he got two yards. He swung the club and caught the man between the neck and shoulder. Whack!

Good shot, Willie, the stick seemed to say.

Why, thank you, stick.

Motherfucker fell, screaming. "Mama-oh shit-daddy!"

Strange relationship his parents must have had, Willie thought. He turned. The second cutter had dropped his saw, too, but he wasn't running. He shambled instead toward Willie, his arms lifted, his big hands clutched into white-knuckled fists. His young face was corneredrat desperate.

Willie admired bravery in an enemy, but Gawd Damn lost big points for dumb, there was more than normal white man stupidity going on here. This fool would dare to attack *him*, Willie, the Lord of the Jungle? Jesus, would they never learn?

Willie ran for the cutter, ducked the awkward, panicked roundhouse punch the man threw and slammed his club into the man's belly. Gawd Damn went, "Uh-hoo!" and doubled up. He fell forward onto the damp ground, forehead first. Willie admired the noise when the cutter hit the soft ground, it was kind of a whumpish thump. Or maybe a thumpish whump.

Willie lowered his club. Enough. The Lord of the Jungle fought clean. The Lord of the Jungle didn't hit 'em when they were down. The Lord of the Jungle didn't kill 'em unless he absolutely had to. They'd live and they'd leave and they'd spread the word not to fuck around in Willie's forest, by God.

Willie took a deep breath, and the sound of his yell bounced once again through the forest, and, naturally, impressed the hell out of all the rabbits and trees and bears who heard it. The yell summed it all up, more or less, into "I'm-Willie-the-Lord-of-the-Jungle-and-I've just-saved-all-your-asses-from-the-evil-white-men-tree-cutters." More or less.

The rabbits and the trees and the bears would be grateful,

Willie knew. It was his job to protect them, their jobs to be grateful. It evened out.

With those thoughts filling his head, Willie loped easily off into the trees. He glanced back once and saw the man with the broken collarbone sit up and moan.

"Motherfucker," the man said softly.

Later, Willie slept soundly in the the cradle of a three-hundred-year-old Douglas fir branch, eighty feet up. It was the sleep of a man good at his work, and as he'd drifted into it, he knew he'd earned it.

"—crew can clean it all out in six months, the goddamned union doesn't call a strike." The speaker was a tall, spindly man with a saltand-pepper beard—no mustache—and exophthalmically bulged eyes. Ichabod Crane in middle age, but named Leroy Haskins; he was the manager of the Callam Bay office.

"What about the Indians?" the second man asked. He was William Parkhurst, and he fiddled with his tie; it was silk, with regimental stripes he'd never earned. He walked to the window and looked out through the dirty glass. Raining again. So what else was new? God, he wasn't cut out for this kind of pressure.

"No problem," Haskins said. "They're still hassling with King over their shutdown. The tribal council isn't going to risk pissing—ah—irritating the only paper company still hiring. Too many men out of work as it is."

Parkhurst nodded. "It would make us look very good to develop a positive cash flow, Leroy. Atlanta would be pleased. But the risks have to be considered. What was that number you came up with?"

"Six million nine," Haskins said. "Counting the Japanese log exports and the pulp deal with Creach."

Parkhurst stroked his tie, thinking about that. Almost seven million dollars. My. With every other division of Multinational Paper currently losing money ass over teakettle, the boys on the fourteenth floor in Atlanta would be very pleased. They'd line up to kiss Parkhurst's cheeks. Both sets.

But.

One had to be cautious, always. Never run when you could walk, never walk when you could crawl, never crawl when you could grovel. That was the basis of Parkhurst's personal and corporate policy and it had served him well for years, it had kept him alive in the shark infested waters. He hated making decisions. Direct action was so...unsettling. There needed to be a committee, a subcommittee, an executive board, feints, subterfuges, and some general beating-aroundthe-bush. To spread the blame around when—God forbid—the shit hit the fan as it was sometimes wont to do. It ought to be taught in every business school in America: Cover-Your-Ass 101.

Parkhurst blinked and stared at Haskins. "What about the environmentalists?"

"Bates is handling that, no problem. A few loose nuts and bolts will protest like always, but the Washington State Legislature knows which side of the bread is buttered. We've been cutting trees here for twenty-nine years; every log truck on the road means dollar signs for the state and they know it."

Parkhurst nodded absently. It would be a simple deal, technically. Almost a straight swap, all that lovely old-growth timber for some useless scenic-view property out by Sekiu.

Six million nine.

Parkhurst sighed. He had the power to do it, all on his own, a quick scrawl of the pen, zip, it was in the works.

But.

If there was a screwup, anywhere, for any reason, it was his ass.

On the other hand...

MacArdle's red face with its Freud-like beard popped into Parkhurst's mind. How could you trust a psychiatrist named

MacArdle? Still, the man was the second most expensive analyst in Seattle, highly regarded and sought after. He'd been Parkhurst's shrink for four years.

"Now, Bill, why is it you don't feel comfortable today?"

"Christ, you're the doctor, Art, you tell me."

"Ah. Avoiding responsibility again, I see. You know you have to take care of your own problems, eventually."

Parkhurst sighed. He knew. Decisions, all the time, decisions. Why couldn't he be a fucking housewife like Marsha? Lie around all day, watching the tube, getting fatter—life wasn't fair.

"It isn't—"

"—fair," MacArdle finished for him. "Come on, let's not do that again, Bill. It's your head, so it's your problem. Or, as we like to say, the Frankenstein Concept of psychoanalysis: you created it, you take care of it." MacArdle smiled.

The son-of-a-bitch—

"—see them?" Haskins said, interrupting Parkhurst's flashback.

The VP blinked. "Uh, yeah. Work up the numbers for me on a graph, use colored pens, and I'll take it back to Seattle."

Well. He could do that much. But should he make a presentation to the boys on the fourteenth floor? Or maybe delegate somebody else to do it? Or should he just spring it on them? Decisions, all the fucking time! There had to be some way to weasel out of it—

Willie shifted on the thick branch and his sense of balance took over. He awoke in plenty of time to keep from rolling ass-first out into empty air. Not even close.

It was cool and dark, a nice late-spring evening. No rain today, that was unusual. Willie settled himself back onto the limb and faded slowly back to sleep . He was master of all he could see and hear and smell. Protector of the rabbits and trees and bears. It was a good feeling.

———

"Come on, Barry, what are you and Jimmy using in those tobacco tins? Not Copenhagen, not with a story like that."

"I'm telling you, Leroy, that's the way it happened!" Barry Lotz was tall, heavy-set, young, and mean. He'd once laid out four men in a bar in Forks for laughing too loud; another time, he'd spun his pickup over the side of Dead Car's Curve and totalled it, only to come up without a scratch, carrying a forty-pound chain saw in each hand and cursing. Barry was nobody's playtoy, no sir.

Right now, though, Barry looked like six miles of dirt road after two days of hard rain and log tricks. Pale as a toadstool bottom. *Scared.*

"He was a short, stubby dude, he had a spare tire around his middle and he was as naked as a fuckin' jaybird. And old, too. He had gray hair all over his crotch—" Barry pronounced it "crouch"—"and he had to be at least fifty."

Barry was twenty-three. Leroy was fifty and he didn't much care for the old man label on somebody his age. "And he came running out of the trees carrying a baseball bat and took you and Jimmy out, bap, just like that? This fat, gray, *old* man?"

"He was fast, Leroy! Before I could do much more than get a look, he whacked Jimmy and came back at me. I went to deck him and he let me have it in the gut with that stick. He bounced around like a goddamned deer! I couldn't breathe for five minutes."

"It's true, Leroy." That was Jimmy Henderson. He sat on a padded black table while the short nurse practitioner put a figure-eight brace over his bare back and shoulders. "Just like Barry said. We heard this awful yell—ow, shit, lady!"

"Sorry," the NP said, pulling the strap tighter. She might be a small woman, but she was strong enough to cinch a broken collarbone into place. And she didn't look sorry.

"He yelled, you said," Leroy prompted.

"Just like fucking Tarzan in the movies. After he finished bashing on us, he did it again. Scared the shit out of me."

Haskins shook his head. That was all he needed. Some loon running around in the woods playing an apeman, kicking the piss out of his loggers. Ah, Jesus.

"Did he look like anybody you know?" Both Jimmy and Barry shook their heads.

"So what we have is a fat old man with no clothes on."

"Well," Barry said, "he was wearing something."

"Oh?"

"Yeah, around his waist. A piece of cloth with stripes on it, the stripes ran like this." He made slashes into the air at a forty-five degree angle.

Leroy shook his head again. Brother.

The receptionist for the NP came into the room. "Telephone, Leroy." It didn't matter that he was the Resident Manager, there was no formality in a town of three hundred people. Haskins went to the phone.

"Haskins? This is Dupuis, in Atlanta."

Leroy sucked in a sudden breath. Fuck, it was old man Doopwee himself! "Sir?"

"Where is William Parkhurst? Seattle says he's still up there in the woods with you. I need to talk to him."

Haskins was surprised. His goggle eyes got a little more so. "No, sir, he left, day before yesterday."

"The hell he did. His plane is still parked at the airport in Port Angeles."

"He left here Tuesday morning in his Continental, Mr. Dupuis, sir, I saw him pull out. He said he was going straight to the airport."

"Has he got a woman out there somewhere?"

Well, yes, there was Becky, but she was working, so that didn't count. "Uh, not that I know of, sir."

"Well, if he doesn't, he didn't make it to the airport for some other reason. Stir up the local law and find him."

"Yes sir, right away Mr. Dupuis sir."

After he cradled the receiver, Haskins stared at the white plastic phone. Oh, Christ, what a mess! First, some kook in the woods, now this. It was not going to be his day.

Suddenly, a flash lit Haskins' brain. It made no sense, at first. He got an image of his boss, Parkhurst, playing with his silk tie. With his striped silk tie. With the strips that ran like *this*.

He got another image, of Barry slashing in the air.

Like this.

Oh, my. Oh, no. It couldn't be.

Even as he thought about how impossible it was, Haskins had another thought: he'd just lied to the President of the Company. Parkhurst *was* still here.

In the woods.

A short, fat, gray man, naked except for a striped piece of cloth around his middle. Like that cloth was a regimentally striped tie, maybe?

Oh, Jesus Fucking Christ.

Willie chewed on the root and watched the three deer. He shook his head to clear away the sudden hot lance of thought which impaled his skull. William Hollis Parkhurst, sir, corporate Vice President, Wood Products Division, Multinational Paper?

No. He wasn't forty-eight years old with gray hair—what was left of it—with thirty pounds of flab that ballooned his body, lapped over his expensive belt and tailored trousers and gave him high blood pressure and low backaches. And *Semi-erectus hardus* for the last three damned years. No way! That was a dream. A nightmare.

The vision faded. Good. He took another bite of the root. It was tough, starchy, and slightly bitter. Didn't matter. He could eat something else. Maybe he could even get one of the deer. Or did they come under his protection? The rabbits and trees and bears did, of course, but deer? Hmm. He'd have to think about that one.

Well, the root was better than the mushrooms, with their dank, dirty-wet taste. Those had been nasty. When had he eaten them? Ah, yes, he remembered. Just after the other bad dream. He'd dreamed he'd been inside a metal-and-glass cage, zooming over a hard path, when the path collapsed. He'd bounced and jostled and jolted inside the cage down the side of a hill, through thin trees until he'd been knocked stupid. When he woke up, it was dark and he was lost. And tired and cold and hungry and it was raining and he was…frightened.

Willie laughed aloud at that memory. Frightened! In *his* woods?

Ha!

But he had been hungry, in the dream, so he'd tried some of the pale brown mushrooms he found growing up from a pile of stinky, cow-pie-like mud. Gah.

Things had gotten very strange in the dream after that.

Still, the bad dream had faded and Willie got back to the business of being who he was: Willie, Lord of the Jungle. Things got clear, a lot of things. All about the white men who were out to cut his forest and machines and dangers and all like that. So Willie took to the trees, naturally, where he felt right at home.

Willie sniffed and caught the scent of a black bear turd. He stood and caught the lowest branch of the alder tree. The bear, being one of his charges, wouldn't bother him, of course, but there might be a male and a female and he didn't want to scare them away, in case they wanted to mate or something. He could watch.

Climbing seemed harder than he remembered and his muscles were sore, but Willie tried to ignore these things. He was after all, the Lord of the Jungle and such things went with the job.

Something was bothering him, though, he couldn't quite put

his finger on it. No matter. It would come to him later, he was sure.

The deputy was an ugly man. He looked a lot like a 1940s movie character called the Creeper. Rondo somebody or other. He said, "Jeez, Leroy, what do you want me to do?"

"What I want you to do, Burt, is find our missing Vice President. And bring him back. Carefully. He must have hit his head or something, he wasn't anywhere around the wrecked car, so maybe he has amnesia or something."

"He sounds like a dangerous fruit-loop to me."

"Now what makes you think that, Burt?"

"Word gets around."

Haskins smiled, but it was to cover his anger. Dammit! Somebody let it out. If Burt knew, everybody in the fucking town must know by now. Half the people in the state. Probably Channel Four and Dan Fucking Rather knew by now. Ah, Jesus, why do you hate me? What'd I ever do to you?

"Look, you can take some of the crew with you, as many as you need. If anything happens to Parkhurst, my tail will be chopped liver. They bring in a new President Manager, where will that leave your cedar scrounging operation?"

The deputy nodded. "Okay, okay. We'll find him, Leroy."

"Carefully, Burt, carefully. Bring him back very carefully."

With all the cunning of the jungle, Willie knew they were after him. Eight, no, nine of them. They bungled their way into his forest, making a racket which would raise a dead slug. Nine men—

Whups. Hold it. Willie sniffed. What was—was that what he thought it was—? He circled around, downwind of them, and sniffed again. Yes! There was no mistake about *that* odor!

One of the nine was a woman.

Willie knew immediately this was a Good Thing. He had no woman and he certainly needed one. The rabbits had mates, the bears had mates—the trees didn't need any—but he, Willie, had none. Which was wrong, since Lords of the Jungle always had mates. As a rule.

He worked his way carefully through the woods, inching quietly through the vines and brush. Not that they could hear him; they wouldn't have heard a bomb with all the noise they were making.

Laughing, talking, stomping about.

"—Jimmy and Barry must have been nipping away at a pint—"

"—rain again, don't it? That's all we need—"

"—fast for you, Becky? I'll be happy to carry you—"

"—walk you into the ground, buddy-boy—"

The last voice was that of the woman. She was dressed like the others, in loose shirt and pants and boots, but her smell left no doubt in Willie's mind. He crept closer.

The problem was simple: he was Willie, Lord of the Jungle, but he wasn't invincible. Or stupid. Eight-to-one, on the ground, straight up, that might be more than even Willie could handle.

He looked around. There was a hand-sized rock half-buried in a clump of electric-green moss by his foot. He dug the rock out. He aimed at a tree to the left of the men and threw, hard. The rock sailed true and smacked into the tree, chunk.

Everybody looked that way.

Everybody except Willie. He leaped up behind the woman, caught her around the waist with one arm, covered her mouth with his other hand, and pulled her back into the cover of the brush.

The others were already running toward the rock he'd thrown.

Good old stupid-blind-deaf white men, they did it every time.

"Mmmmuuhh!" The woman struggled, but Willie had her.

He could feel her tight, muscular buttocks working against him. She kicked and tried to twist away, but she was wasting her time against the strength of Willie.

Against the hardness of Willie.

"Where the hell is Becky?"

"I don't know, she was right here—"

"Becky!"

"Oh, damn—"

The woman struggled briefly at the beginning, but Willie was persistent. Very persistent.

Four times already he had persisted.

She was a slippery, hot, strong woman, and it was a little awkward on the narrow tree branch eighty feet up, but all in all, it was fine. When her smell told Willie she was ready again, he reached over and touched her. Willie was ready, Willie was rampant, Willie was tempered steel, which was as it should be.

"Oh," she said, as she reached her peak for the fifth time. "Oh, yes!"

She looked much better without her clothes, Willie saw. A natural blond, too, he saw.

Afterwards this time, she smiled. "It wasn't anything like this before, Mr. Parkhurst. You been taking vitamins, or what?"

"Willie," Willie said, touching his chest.

"Well, I hope you remember that I'm Becky and that we've done this before, only not anything at *all* like this."

Willie nodded. Somehow, that didn't seem quite how it was supposed to go, but it was close enough, he guessed. He didn't remember exactly how it was supposed to go, anyhow. But he knew where this thing down between his legs went. He reached for her.

"You ought to be in a circus," she said. But she giggled and held him tightly.

When he finished this time, Willie leaned back and cupped his hands around his mouth and did the yell. Uhhh-ahuh ahuh-ah-uh ahuhah-uh!" This translated loosely to, "Six times, everybody!"

The rabbits and trees and bears all stopped what they were doing.

Those with heads shook them, impressed as hell. Those with bark and leaves just smiled inwardly as only they can, but all in all, everyone was pretty much blown away.

Half a mile into the forest, eight white men suddenly had the shit scared out of them.

"Gone? What the fuck do you mean, 'Gone'?" Haskins's eyes looked ready to pop from his head and drop onto his desktop— a thing which would have given truth to many a malapropism, but it didn't happen.

"Uh…"

"Dammit, man—!"

"We—uh—found her clothes," somebody said.

Haskins stared at the deputy, who looked uglier than ever. "Jesus Christ, man, I send you to find Parkhurst and you fucking *lose* my only woman forester?" EEO would scream, he could already hear them. Another case of blatant discrimination. Why couldn't Parkhurst be queer? Nobody would miss a logger, they were like fleas, but his only woman…

"We figure Parkhurst has got her, she is okay, probably."

Haskins wanted to scream. "Stark naked in the woods with a crazy man who thinks he is fucking *Tarzan* and *you* think she's okay? You fucking moron!"

Haskins reached for his phone. His plans of retiring as a respected corporate officer were rapidly going down the toilet. He knew when he was out of his depth.

He called Seattle.

Normally, corporate wheels ground slowly, but not this time. No, this time, they ground like the Indy 500. This time, the Flash would have had trouble keeping up. In six hours, there were people swarming all over the Callam Bay office. There arrived: the second-highest paid psychiatrist in Seattle; a pair of big-game hunters from Canada; a primate expert from the San Diego Zoo, by way of Tarzana; and twenty Washington state troopers.

Multinational already had an image problem, what with all the scalped hills they'd clearcut in the last few years. If the news media found out about this so many heads would roll they'd have to import a herd of guillotine just to keep up. It was a bad day at black rock here. It was break out the lifeboats and hope they'd float on a sea of shit time.

A special assistant to President Dupuis had even flown up from Atlanta, no mean feat in six hours, and he stood around like something from a Haitian cemetery. Haskins couldn't be sure, but he thought he'd seen fangs when the man smiled, the one time he'd moved his lips.

It was dark, but first thing in the morning, all those people were, by God, going out to find Mr. Parkhurst and Rebecca Lea Copes. And bring them back alive.

Becky snuggled closer to Willie and smiled in her sleep. Under the moon's ghostly gleam, Willie himself was having trouble sleeping. Damned dreams again.

"—process cannot be delegated on this level—"
"—cost-risk is good, save for the foreign—"
"—excuses! Make a decision and stick to it—"

"—no drive, no guts, you have to get tough—"
"—parameters of the overall scenario show—"
"—marketing research indicates—"
"—can't see how—"
"—no, I—"
"—Willie!"

Willie jerked awake and stared out from the safety of the tree—

Safety of the tree? What the hell was he doing in a tree?
The sudden surge passed. Only a dream, Willie, he told himself. Whoee.
Sometimes it wasn't easy being Lord of the Jungle.

He heard them just after sunrise, coming through the woods, a lot of them. Willie nudged Becky awake.
"Huh? What is it? I—oh, God!" She stared at empty space and suddenly latched onto Willie's leg. It took a few seconds to remember.
"Got to go," Willie said, begrudging the words. "Men coming."
Becky yawned. She scratched her left breast; the nipple stood up. "Um. Okay, honey, this is your show."

She climbed pretty well, Willie noticed, as he looked up and watched Becky come down. And looked very good from this angle right beneath her, too.
No time for that now, Willie, get moving.
But—why? Another bad dream reached out and nailed Willie. He looked down and saw his paunch, his bare body, scraped in a dozen places by branches and rough tree bark. And

his dick, that was red and sore, too. My God, what was he doing here? Who was this naked woman smiling at him? Oh, yeah, right, Becky something, the forester he'd slept with a couple of times, but—where were his clothes? Was this something kinky she'd cooked up or what?

There was a mental jumble; his thoughts bounced and rolled and smacked into each other, and, mercifully, the dream faded.

"Come on," Willie said, taking his woman's hand.

They ran.

"Tracks, eh?" one of the Canadian hunters said.

"Fresh, eh?" the other Canadian said. He had the arm and shoulder of a competition curler, which he was. And the brain of a curling stone, too, Haskins thought.

The psychiatrist, dressed in bush khaki from Abercrombie & Fitch, smiled. He spoke briefly into a small recorder he carried. All material for the next book.

The primate expert poked at a dropping near the base of the big alder tree.

"Feces," he said.

Haskins stared at the primate expert. "I brought you all the way out here from San Diego so you could tell me that stinking pile there is shit? Jesus, man—"

"I hate to interrupt your scatalogical research," President Dupuis' assistant said in a voice that would freeze molten steel, "but it looks as if they went that way. Shall we?"

Haskins was sure the man had fangs, look at them! but he wasn't going to point that out to anybody. He knew who had the vulnerable throat here. He nodded. They all went in that direction.

Willie was moving much slower than he wanted. Becky wasn't used to running barefoot and bare-assed through the woods.

"Can't we take a rest, Willie?"

Willie didn't think that was a good idea, but he could see she was tired. So they stopped.

Becky flopped down onto a mat of fir needles. She came up just as fast. "Ouch, crap! I wish you'd let me keep my pants!" She rubbed her rear, then plucked something long and skinny from her pubic thatch.

Willie smiled. She would learn. Once she'd been in the jungle as long as he had—

His brain rumbled and quaked. As long as you have been in the jungle? Listen up, Ace, you've only been here for three days.

Willie shook his head. Something wrong here. He was Willie, Lord of the Jungle, he'd been here his whole life—

Dummy! You're William Parkhurst, Vice President, Multinational Paper, Wood Products, timber, like that. And weasel. Crawfish. Waffle. Old, let's-decide-later Bill, remember?

No! Willie shook his head harder. I'm the Lord of the Jungle! Wait. Listen to this: he raised his hands, cupped them around his mouth, took a deep breath. "Uh—" That was as far as he got. His great cry, the yell which always blew the rabbits and trees and bears away, the sound which scared the shit out of white men, sputtered into a hacking cough.

"Willie?"

Willie looked at Becky.

William Parkhurst's eyes opened wide. Willie started to reassure his new mate.

William Parkhurst's voice took over. "My God!"

The sounds of the men tromping through the trees reached them. Willie felt a stab of alarm. William Parkhurst felt a surge of relief.

The dichotomy of minds twirled and the single body ached trying to pull the two together. Which was the dream and which was real? God, William Parkhurst thought, what the hell is going on here? Wrongness, Willie thought. Bad things here.

Twirling and swirling, the two minds banged against each

other, fighting to survive, clawing at each other like starved animals in a cage.

Something had to give. Something did.

The group of men charged into the clearing. Becky stared at Willie. It was a slow-motion film, a morning mired in molasses.

And when the thing going on within the mind of the naked man with the tie around his waist finally stopped, he became something different from what he had been.

He *fused*.

"Mr. Parkhurst?" Leroy Haskins said.

"Bill?" the psychiatrist said.

"Just call me Willie," Willie said. Not that he was Willie of the Jungle anymore. Somebody else would have to protect the rabbits and trees and bears from now on, now that Willie understood who he really was. No more namby-pamby shifting for him, no more weasel or crawfish or later—Bill, no way. He knew who he was, now. He knew.

He grinned a wide and happy grin. He was going to be scaring the shit out of a lot of white men directly. They didn't have a chance.

He was Willie of the *Corporate* Jungle now, and he had bigger fish to fry.

The boys in Atlanta were in for a little surprise, they were.

Uhhh-ahuhahuh-ah-uh-ahuhah-uh, Willie thought. But he kept it to himself.

For now.

Clearance to Land

ADAM-TROY CASTRO

Introduction

"Clearance To Land" is Adam-Troy Castro's first published story. When it landed on my desk, it was in paper (yes, this was the dark ages), printed in tiny type with a faded dot matrix printer. For those of you who can't imagine that, the words were too small to see well and they were a light gray.

I figured it would take me five seconds, tops, to reject this story. Instead, I found myself on page three before I surfaced enough to move to a part of my office with better lighting so I could give the manuscript a fair read.

I have a hunch that no other editor took the time to glance at the manuscript. This story is so compelling, even with its stylistic oddities—or maybe because of them—that it's impossible to put down.

After this sale, Adam has gone on to publish more than twenty-six novels, more short stories than I can count, and quite a bit of nonfiction. He won the Philip K. Dick award and the Seiun Award, which is also known as the Japanese Hugo. His work has been nominated for eight Nebulas, three Stokers, two Hugos, and, internationally, the Premios Ignotus (Spain), the Grand Prix de l'Imaginaire (France), and the Kurd-Laßwitz Preis (Germany).

And this is where it all began.

Clearance to Land

Adam-Troy Castro

You are forty-seven years old

and you have back trouble, and you do not bend easily, and the edge of your belt buckle jabs at your belly like a dull blade

and you are desperately tired, but too scared of death to sleep

and your feet, which are the only things you've been allowed to look at for hours now, are tingling so madly from lack of circulation that you ache for permission to stamp them

but the bearded man is a cruel bastard, and has more than once punished frivolous requests with violent beatings

and so you grimace, and you press your head further than you thought possible into the empty space between your knees, and you look at your shoes, which are resting on carpeting sticky from dried blood, and you listen hopelessly for the sound of another murder

but at the moment, nobody is dying loud enough for you to hear them. The engines continue the droning hum audible from every seat in the plane; your daughter coughs under her breath every two or three minutes, to clear that congenitally dry throat of hers; paper rustles, from God knows where, somewhere behind you; somebody three or four aisles away whispers a couple of words to his neighbor, and manages to get away with it, this time; and the blood roars in your ears, like a trapped beast

but nobody's dying. Nobody's being shot in the chest. Nobody's being stabbed in the throat. Nobody's being bludgeoned to death with the butt of a semi-automatic rifle. Nobody's being murdered. And the reason for that is simple: nobody's moving. They're doing what you're doing: sitting on the edge of their seats, with their heads between their knees, and their hands clasped together behind their heads. They're ignoring the pain in their backs and the dizziness from lack of movement and the stench rising from their unwashed bodies, and they're going mad with fear

as they've been doing ever since you left American airspace, when the bearded man stood up in his seat; when you somehow knew, even before his bald partner came running down the aisle, everything he was going to say

. . .

and it didn't seem fair to you, then, because this was happening to you already. That was why you were on this damn plane. You were on this plane because your daughter was on this plane, and your daughter was on this plane because two days earlier your son-in-law, in Paris on a business trip, was blown to shreds by a firebomb that went off in a fast food restaurant, and she needed to pick up what was left of the body. The very idea that this could happen in your life two times in one week had seemed insane to you at the time

and ever since then you've wondered just how many of the surviving passengers still regard this as a mere hijacking. At least a tenth, you suppose. Maybe. People are that way. Faced with something impossible, something that becomes more and more impossible with every passing second, they focus on the concrete threat: the bald man and his sadistic bearded partner. They take what the bald man said for granted. This is a hijacking. Right. Cooperate and you won't be hurt. Sure. We want to exchange you for political prisoners. Uh huh. We believe you. We've all seen this kind of thing happening on the news; we may have never believed it would happen to us, but we know it happens to somebody, somewhere, and it might as well be us. This sort of thing is easy to believe in. Easier than the rest of it, anyway. The rest of it is downright impossible. And you ache to know just how many of your fellow passengers have managed to deny

what your daughter's known for a long time. Her eyes are black dots on a doughy white face, and the perspiration seems to be rolling off her body in waves and you're pretty sure that the impossibility of your situation has driven her insane. You'd know for sure, one way or another, if you could only get a substantial look at her, but it's been hours since you've been able to get her to meet your eyes. The last time was—when? this morning?—when the bald man ordered all the window shades lowered. As one of the passengers unfortunate enough to be sitting next to a window, you were permitted to raise your head for all of a second and a half; and you took advantage of that trivial second and a half of freedom to look at your daughter. She was looking past you, at the window sliding shut behind you. Her face was red from the light shining through the glass, then white from the normal electric light of the cabin, then shadowed as the bald man screamed that it was time for everybody to bend over again. Her eyes met yours then, for just a fraction of a second, and there was damned little sanity left in them. There must be less left there now. And you know how she feels. You're so far gone that it's been easily two, maybe three hours since you remembered that the bag of dry blood slumped in the seat between you and your daughter was once your wife

and though you know you should feel grief, or shock, or something like that, you feel nothing. You've always feared having to watch something horrible happen to somebody you loved, and you've always loved your wife, more or less. The affection the two of you felt for each other was never the passionate, all-consuming thing they write about in romances (it was never more than a mildly pleasant affection, at most) but still, you know you should have felt more than a thump of sympathetic pain when the bearded man blew her brains out the back of her head. Of course, by then, you had already realized that something impossible was happening

by then the skies had already begun to take on an improbable reddish hue; by then everything in the cabin was already the color of blood; by then the number to total executions had already left double digits; and by then you'd decided, like just about everybody on the plane, that nobody was going to get out of this alive anyway

but you should still feel more. You should feel hatred. You should want to blind the bastards with your thumbs, and castrate them with your fingernails. You shouldn't be sitting here, head between your knees, obediently staring at the tops of your shoes, for hours on end, feeling only your backache and the tingling of your feet

and it stopped being merely "...hours on end..." almost two weeks ago, didn't it? It sure did. It's been days on end, now. You know this because ever since the beginning, even since the bald one whimsically ordered everybody into crash positions, your wristwatch has been in clear view. It's an analog watch, of course; you learned how to read a clock at six years of age and you've always considered digitals a form of cheating. It was just about midnight, on a Friday, when the hijacking began; by the time the hour hand was pointing straight up again, twelve hours later, two stewardesses were dead and your greatest concern was that the plane would run out of fuel before the hijackers found a country that would give them permission to land. Your wife was still alive, then, though gripping your hand so tightly that her fingernails drew blood; your daughter was still managing to throw you an occasional brave smile, though they were as transparent as tissue paper; and you still believed that this was just a hijacking, albeit an extraordinarily brutal one, and one you stood scant chance of walking away from. By the time the hour hand rotated all the way back to twelve, seven more people, including three children from one family, were rotting in their seats; the view outside the window was disconcertingly pink; your daughter was asleep; your wife was sobbing quietly; and the only thought in your mind was *dammit, where's all the fuel coming from?* Then the hour hand made another full rotation, and

it was twelve hours later, and the plane still hadn't landed anywhere to refuel, and it was still flying, and the sky was the color of blood, and nobody had had anything to eat, and nobody had had anything to drink, and nobody had been to the bathroom, and nobody had needed to do any of these things, and you saw in your wife's eyes, and in your daughter's eyes, and in the eyes of the other passengers, that they knew this was beyond possibility, that they wanted someone else to tell them that they were merely insane. And the bearded man, who never seemed to sit down, marched down the aisle, and shot a college student dead just to prove he was still capable of doing it, and the passengers looked at their own feet again. The hour hand made another full rotation

and a woman in the next section up went crazy. She just stood up in her seat—ignoring her husband, who frantically grabbed at her—and started screaming that this was going on forever, that this was never going to end, that somebody had to do something, that somebody had to make it stop. Her head was in fragments before she said the word stop. And the hour hand made another full rotation. And another full rotation after that. And an eighth. And an eleventh. And a seventeenth. And a twenty first, and

there's no reason to dwell on all of that, when all of that is clearly impossible, since the bearded man is walking up your aisle again. You don't see him, of course; you're still obediently looking at your feet. But you can hear him coming, and you don't need to see him to know

. . .

he's pointing the machine gun at every head he passes. He's frowning. He's running his black tongue over the surface of his black little lips. His lips are the color and consistency of a dog's. His pores are big and wet. His beard is moist. He's blinking. He's restless. He's bored. His footsteps are getting closer. He's stopping. And

suddenly you know he's looking at you. Or your daughter. And you close your eyes tighter than they've ever been closed in your entire life, so tight it hurts, and you feel the part of you that still cares pray *let it be me, not my daughter.* And eons pass. And you feel him lean over you, and you feel something cold and metallic press hard against your temple, and the part of you that still cares turns selfish and evil and thinks, *no, I was wrong, let it be anybody else,* and

the bearded man says, "Come with me,"

and there's an immediate stir among the other passengers, because up until now the bearded man hasn't been interested in anything other than killing people. Something else is going to happen now. It's unquestionably something worse—everybody knows the bearded man well enough by now to know that it can't be something better—but at least it's something else. And it's happening to you, first. And

you're so stunned not only to be alive, but to be the one person, out of the few dozens remaining alive, to be chosen to break the pattern, that for a moment you don't move. You don't even look up. You just remain frozen, waiting for the other shoe to drop. For him to change his mind and pull the trigger. But when he says, "Come with me" a second time, with the deadly impatience of a man to whom other people are easily disposable commodities, you jerk upright at once, eager to show him just how willing you are to obey. Too quickly. The blood drains from your head. Your knees buckle. The world goes gray. You almost collapse. You force yourself to look into his eyes

and even with the few pitiful glances you've been able to manage now and then, when he wasn't looking directly at you, you've been able to tell that there was something seriously wrong with his eyes, but now you see what it is. They're not eyes. They're

what eyes look like, on photographic negatives: white irises surrounded by football-shaped fields of black. The pupils are so bright that by the time you blink, a purple afterimage has been left on your retina. You gasp. You think *there's fire in there*

and then his hand shoots forward and grabs you by the collar and pulls you toward him. He pulls you past the corpse that was once your wife and the cringing wreck that was once your daughter; and when along the way a cold hand closes on yours, there's one truly terrible moment when you think the hand belongs to your wife

but no, it's your daughter; there's life in her yet; she doesn't want him to take you, and she's trying, however feebly, to hold you back. You wish her the strength to manage it, as if strength alone would do any good. But you're yanked from her grip so easily the bearded man doesn't even notice she tried to interfere

and he places you on your feet in the center of the aisle. And he says, "Walk." And for the first time in almost thirteen days you walk. You're out of practice. Your feet don't approach the ground at the right angle. They hit glancingly, on the edges. You stumble. You limp. You have to keep an eye on them to make sure they're doing what you want them to be doing. And even so they try to trick you; once or twice you find yourself veering to the left or right. But you walk on, because the bearded man is following you. You can't hear him, because right now you can't hear anything except the bass drum in your chest; but you can feel him, because the ache in the center of your back feels exactly like a wound, and the hollow at the base of your spine is filling up with puddled sweat that feels exactly like blood

and you can see him, because some of the surviving passengers are stealing glimpses at you as you pass them. Most of those seem to hate you. They quickly meet your eyes, hostility burning in their otherwise hopeless faces, and then they look at their feet, before the bearded man sees the expression directed at him. Others seem to be pleading for you to do something, though what they expect you to do is a mystery. And then there are the dead, some of whom have complete faces; they glare at you with contempt, murmuring, "Too Late, Too Late, Too Late." You offer no responses to any of them. You can't. Just walking, without collapsing in a heap and thus surrendering yourself to the inevitable bullet in the back, is as much as you can manage. And so you walk forward—

. . .

past the stewardesses who lie sprawled in the galleys, the children who sit sobbing next to dead parents, the blood-splattered old woman who could be either alive or dead, but whose expression, of nearly infinite shock and grief, makes either possibility equally horrible

—and as you walk, it gradually becomes clear to you that you're walking uphill. That the nose of the plane is elevated. That you feel unnaturally light. That the steady drone of rushing wind is growing louder. That, after twelve and a half days, the plane has at last reached final approach

(to what?)

and as you pass the spiral staircase leading up to First Class, the bearded man taps you on the shoulder and says, "Up." What can you do? You climb up. The weakness in your legs, combined with the clumsiness of fear and the slight but definitely perceptible tilt of the stairway, turns the fourteen steps into an impossibly difficult climb. When you stop to squeeze the handrail, as if to confirm that it's still there, the barrel of the bearded man's rifle bumps against the back of your knees, and again he says, "Up." You take a step up. And then another one. And then another one after that. And your head emerges into First Class. The faces of the First Class passengers swivel as one to greet you

shocking both you and them. You're pale and terrified and splattered with blood and brains; they're pale and terrified but clean and, without even a single exception, alive and well. They gasp when they see you; this is the first time they've seen somebody from down below, and they now know, in a small way, what all the shots were about. You try to tell them everything with a look

help, you say with your eyes, they're killing everybody, there's no end to it, please do something, he can't kill everybody if we all just rush him at once

but once again the rifle barrel prods you at the base of the spine, and once again the bearded man says "Up," and you proceed upward

into the cockpit

which is so dimly lit that, at first, you mistakenly interpret what you see as thick electrical cables, pulled from the machinery for some reason and crisscrossed about the room like streamers. Each is the width of a child's arm, and each is anchored to one of the seats where the members of the flight crew sit. Their shadows cavort on the curved ceiling. You look down, searching for the light source, which seems to be coming from someplace near the floor, and you find it immediately: a single red candle, standing in a puddle of melted wax. The plane shakes. You look up. The cables are swinging back and forth like jump rope. One of them swings close to your face, and you catch a whiff of something you've smelt before

—most notably a few months ago, when one of the sewer lines in your office building broke open and spilled several gallons of human excrement all over the men's room. The stink hadn't been quite this bad, back then—

. . .

and even back then, it had been more than you were able to stand. This time the stench hits you like a physical blow. You gag, and close your eyes, and try to double over. In another second you'll vomit. The bearded man grabs you by the back of the collar and pulls you upright. You try to say, "Please." He won't let you do that either. He pushes you into the room. You duck one of the swinging cables, skid on a slippery spot, and take a step forward. There's not much to see here; the indicator lights on the instruments are all off, rendering the entire console invisible, and the windshield itself is hidden by an expanse of black cloth that covers it like curtains. The flight crew is

dead, of course. There are four of them. Three lie sprawled in their chairs, arms swinging bonelessly at their sides. Their faces, dangling backwards over the tops of their chairs, stare at you upside down with the cold contemptuous indifference of the dead, candlelight dancing in their glazed eyes. In death, they seem to recognize you, in a way you've never been able to recognize yourself, and they seem to be taking a vague pleasure in refusing to tell you about it. You swallow. The fourth sits in the captain's seat, with his hands on the controls; and the second you decide that this one is not dead after all

he turns to greet you. It's the bald man. He smiles at you, with glistening teeth. "Hello," he says, and waits for a reply. And just as you realize that the thick ropy things draped about the cabin are not electrical cables

(you have to press your hand against the control console to keep yourself from collapsing in shock; it's metallic, but it's warm, and it presents for you the only remaining solid surface in the entire universe)

the bald man, oblivious, says, "We're about to land, and we've chosen you to help us with the exchange." Just like that. In this room, his words are like distant babble, in no language known to man. You force yourself to focus on tone instead of meaning, the bland face instead of the atrocity it's committed, and, just barely, manage to choke a reply: what exchange? "The prisoner exchange," he says, as if that's obvious. The phrase means nothing to you. He sees your confusion and elaborates: "The authorities have finally agreed to our demands." What authorities? What demands? You feel yourself trying to faint, but there's no place to sit: all the chairs are occupied by eviscerated corpses. You wonder if they know what's happened to them. You wonder what it's like to be treated like an envelope made out of skin, to be opened up like a letter and have your contents removed and displayed around the room like wall decorations. You wonder if he brought you here to do the same thing to you. The bald man frowns impatiently. "We're not terrorists," he says, seeming to need your agreement. "We're freedom fighters. We're fighting a fight that needs to be fought." You nod dully, eager to please him, eager to show him just how anxious you are to cooperate. Disappointed but apparently not angry, he dismisses you with a wave of his hand, and turns his attention back to the controls. The bearded man behind you claps you on the shoulder and says, "Down,"

to the First Class section, where he places you in an empty seat opposite a pretty young woman in a starched white suit. Her face is tightly locked in the kind of expression fussy hostesses wear when an oafish guest uses the wrong fork by mistake. And it seems to be directed at you

151

. . .

which takes you a moment to understand. Unlike you, she's been safely, if only slightly, insulated, from the bloodshed of the lower decks. And she's been able to place it at the correct emotional distance. Like all these others. You glance at the others—

the priest, the old woman with the bright red lipstick, the cherubic fat man who requires two seats, and the rest

—and though they don't look at you, because they don't want to be caught staring, you can see the same revulsion toying at the corners of their mouths as well. You wonder what it's been like for them, these past two weeks. Oh, they were probably terrified enough, at least at first

but soon enough they noticed that none of their own were being killed, and they decided that the slaughter taking place elsewhere, though a real shame, had nothing to do with them personally. They took comfort in that. They've grown bored. Until you, their first reminder that the massacre has a human face, had the colossal bad taste to intrude upon their antiseptic refuge. Part of you can understand how they feel: two weeks ago, confronted with a figure that reeked of death as powerfully as you do now, you would have shrunken away yourself. You would have done anything to escape him. But the rest of you feels a sudden overwhelming hate for these privileged ones. How dare they sit up here, snug and secure in their luxurious carpeted womb, and pass judgment on you? How dare they look disgustedly at you, when their families are whole and alive and no blood stains their expensive clothes? And how dare they look pretty and clean as they daintily avert their eyes from the gore that's been drowning you? You open your mouth to scream at them, but you don't get the chance, because

all around you

from outside the plane

a sound like a hundred babies being mauled by iron knives. Like a thousand cats being plunged into boiling water. Like a million men having their lower jaws ripped from their faces. Like a billion drill bits being activated inside a billion skulls. Like

nothing you've ever heard, to tell the truth, but it's a sound you recognize immediately, because it's a sound you've known since your conception, even if until now you haven't allowed yourself to know that you knew it. It's

the sound that's been going on forever, in the place you've just landed

the sound of the place that up until thirteen days ago was your greatest fear in the whole world; the place they told you you might end up, the place they preached about in Sunday School

and you can't fly a hijacked plane to the afterlife, but somehow the bald man has managed it

. . .

"to free political prisoners," the bald man had said

and as the dilettantes of First Class recognize the sound too, the knowledge hits them with the force of a sledgehammer, and they sink deep into their seats, as if each and every one of them was suddenly three or four times heavier. They're shattered, all of them. You feel your own guts turn to liquid, but you've spent the past couple of weeks hearing a pale imitation of that sound, in the form of senseless slaughter, and you're able to manage a small and inadequate reaction. You start to stand. You start to say something. You have no idea what you're about to do or about to say

and you don't have the chance to find out, because the bearded man is back. He pulls you into the aisle for the second time in ten minutes, looks you over to make sure you still possess at least a small percentage of your innate faculties, and says, "We've landed." And around you, the screaming starts

affecting the bearded man not at all. He looks around idly, his face passing over the elegant old woman, the priest, the fat man, the middle-aged marrieds, the couple with the baby

and apparently deciding to do the easiest one first, places his cold dark hand on the shoulder of the pretty young woman you'd just decided to despise, and says, "Help her downstairs,"

and you comply, because there's a machine gun at your back, and nothing can make a human being march another human being into hell better than a machine gun at his back. You place a hand under her elbow and gently pull her to her feet. She doesn't possess the strength to stand. She collapses against you, clutching at the lapels of your jacket, sobbing that there must have been a mistake, that they must have mistaken her for someone else, that she'd never done anything to deserve this. "Hurry her up," says the bearded man. "We've got a lot of comrades to free." You pull her into the aisle. She screams louder, but doesn't resist; she just walks with you, helplessly, as if her feet are not her own, as if what she does with them is no longer any of her business. She lets you escort her to the stairway. She lets you make her start descending the stairs. She doesn't try to escape when her position two stairs lower than yourself makes it impossible for you to maintain a strong grip. She doesn't shudder when the bearded man steps onto the stairway after you. She just screams, continuously; and

halfway down the stairs you almost join her. The front hatch, the one which had been connected to the tunnel which had been connected to the terminal which had been connected to the real world, is open. And beyond it churns a sea of molten rock, a sea that crashes and boils and flares as violently as the surface of the sun, and a sea where the loudest sound is the wailing of unseen millions of people. The heat from the open door raises blisters on your skin. You can't force yourself to get any closer than the bottom of the stairway. But the bearded man shoves you and your terrified charge aside, walks right up to the door without any apparent discomfort, sticks his head out, and producing a megaphone from somewhere, shouts: "First prisoner!" And, grabbing the shrieking young woman by the arm

hurls her out the hatch like a doll. Somehow, she manages to turn around in mid-plunge to face you

. . .

and her expression, all eyes and all mouth, doesn't possess even a shred of hope in it. It's the face of someone who no longer needs hope, or sanity. It's the face of someone unjustly damned. Even as she turns, her clothes have turned to ash and dropped away; her hair is beginning to smolder; her skin is beginning to dance with flame. The ground beneath her is already starting to reach upward, in the shape of a clawed six-fingered hand, to claim her. You catch a glimpse of fire beginning to catch on her tongue

before the fingers close

and you become aware that there's a body at your feet: a body that wasn't there a second ago—the body of a naked man a shade above five feet tall. Horribly blackened and burned, still smoking from the fires that have just released him, and twitching uncontrollably, the only part of him recognizably human is his face, which the flames have left untouched. He looks like nobody special—olive-skinned, brown-eyed, with a big nose and a fine lattice of what to you seems to be acne scars, he could be anybody. You glance up at the bearded man, who flashes the kind of rictus grin that only appears on the faces of electrocuted prisoners, and says the burned man's name. The burned man weeps in response

and as the bearded man disappears up the circular stairway, you can do nothing but listen to the screams. Not the ones from upstairs, of course, or even the ones now coming from the aft sections—

. . .

they're still audible, the way a flute is still audible in the middle of a symphony

—but the screams outside the plane. They're screams of a different color entirely. Screams that have attained an awful power that you've never heard in screams before. Screams that make the screams of your fellow passengers sound like weak moans. And though there are millions of them, they don't blend together; somehow, each and every individual voice among that vast chorus remains wholly audible by itself. Each scream retains its own character, and each scream is totally discordant with all the rest. The woman from First Class is still there, of course, and her scream is awful because it's the scream of a new arrival, who is still beginning to understand that this is all she has to look forward to, forever; but surrounding her on all sides are the screams of people who have been here so long that they can't remember anything else, and their screams are immeasurably worse. In between are screams that still contain words. Most are in languages you don't recognize. Others are voices you have a sick feeling you recognize. They're people you used to know, years ago; most of them are people you didn't like, but you didn't hate them, you didn't want to torture them, you didn't want to see them dance in a furnace for your amusement. You want to apologize to them for not joining them in their agony. And you want to do something—anything at all, the specifics don't matter—for them, but

instead you sit where you are and do nothing as the bearded man marches another helpless hostage to the hatchway. This one's the fat priest. Unlike the young woman, he's struggling. He's kicking and biting and, dammit, he's drawing blood. The bearded man is bleeding from the nose. The bearded man is missing a bite-sized gob of flesh from his right arm. The bearded man is having trouble controlling him. But he's still the stronger of the two: inch by inch, millimeter by millimeter, the priest is still being backed up toward the door. He jabs the bearded man in the belly. The bearded man grunts and shoves him onward. The priest's eyes dart toward you. You feel the impulse to move

but your legs remain frozen. The priest is back up against the hatch now. His leg dangles over the inferno; smoke begins to rise from his black pants leg. You can't look away, but you can't move either. And then fingers as brittle as autumn leaves circle your wrist

and pull you down against your will

to face the eyes of the burnt man. They're surprisingly bright, and filled with both infinite anger and infinite will to enforce it. He despises you. He hates the rawness of your flesh and the naiveté in your soul, and if his arms weren't charcoaled sticks fresh from the campfire he'd gladly peel the features from your stupid face, but

there's fear there, too, coupled with such desperation that for a moment you forget the machine guns and the blood and the millions of screams and move closer to the burnt man of your own accord, to hear what he has to say

and he opens his lips and he coughs out a cloud of glowing embers

• • •

and, with breath the odor of burnt meat, he begs you to stop it

he tells you that nobody deserves to be tortured forever; that nobody deserves to be held in the grip of infinite power and infinite sadism; that he can't stand to see anybody thrown into the fire; and he says all this in a language you don't recognize, but even so you understand every word

but even as he begs you again to please, please, do something to stop it the chorus of screamers outside the plane increases by one, and there's another burnt man at your feet. This one materializes face down, though you're unable to tell that at first, because he's so swollen from the heat that one side of him looks the same as the other. But then he turns over, without any help from you, leaving a greasy stain on the carpet where his skin had been touching it

and he peers into your face with dark black eyes set deep on an ugly little face

and he shouts at you impatiently

and you recognize him at once

and you make an incoherent noise, and back away, until the cold metal of one of the seats cuts into your back, and you collapse at its side, helpless to do anything but watch him

．　．　．

no tears for this one. No remorse. None at all. He's not even surprised to be rescued. If anything, he's annoyed that it's taken so long. He's anxious to start over where he left off. And he wants to know what's holding up the return trip. And he shouts all of this at the top of his lungs, the same way he did in all those scratchy old recordings, and his delivery hasn't lost any of its power or charisma for its time spent in the flames. Unlike the first burnt man, he's not a shell of what he was; if anything, he's even more than he was. He just needed to be cooked a little more, that's all; he was a shade underdone before, that's all

and he sees these thoughts on your face, and he extends one blackened and oozing hand as far as it will go and starts pulling himself toward you, leaving a trail of soot on the carpet behind him, and there's clear purpose in his face, and you don't know what's so special about you personally that this murderer of millions has to take care of you himself, but by now you want to die, so it doesn't matter

and the bearded man comes down the stairs again, this time cradling the baby

using both arms, and cooing at it; the machine gun is strapped to the belt at his side. He takes a couple of steps toward the hatchway, winding up for a toss. This is going to be a great throw. The baby is going to sail forty feet before starting to fall

and then the bearded man stops. He looks at the carpeted floor. He follows the trail of soot. He does a double-take when he sees what the new arrival is doing. It's a very theatrical double-take. Its straight out of the movies. He looks impressed. He looks at you, expecting you to share the joke. You can't; you're too busy cringing

so he dismisses you and takes a step toward the hatch and then he stops

and he adds his own voice to the chorus of screams

because the first burnt man, the one you'd first mistaken for an Arab, has shot across the floor like a snake and, with one convulsive squeeze of his clawlike hand

closed around the bearded man's ankle like a vise

and the skin breaks, the bone turns to powder, the calf above the break starts to bulge from dammed blood

and still the burnt man squeezes, until his hand becomes a closed first, and the foot below the bearded man's ankle simply

separates

and as the bearded man shrieks and falls, he drops the baby and clutches at the machine gun latched to his belt, but he can't move anywhere near fast enough—

. . .

the burnt man is already on top of him, seizing it and throwing it, so it lands almost exactly halfway between you and the mass murderer crawling toward you

—and the bearded man is begging now, because the burnt man is pushing him across the floor, toward the hatchway, where the flames are jumping, and the heat is building, and the voices of suffering millions have suddenly become almost musical, almost joyful

and the mass murderer stalking you grabs the machine gun by the barrel, his brittle blackened hands making shiny marks on the metal

and the bearded man is dangling from the hatchway now, holding on with his arms, and you can't see much of him, because most of him is hanging over the fire, but you can see that his hair is beginning to smoke and there are pinpoints of flame beginning to build on the surface of his eyes, and the burnt man is peeling away his grip, finger by trembling finger

and you realize that somehow your finger has encircled the trigger

and as the red glow streaming in through the open hatchway momentarily becomes much, much brighter, the chorus of screams outside the plane becomes louder by one

. . .

and you squeeze the trigger, and the chorus of screams outside becomes louder by yet one more

and you meet the burnt man's eyes

and again, without saying a single word in any language you understand, he tells you about climbing a mountain when he was little, with friends; considering it a game; and it was a tall mountain and he was smaller than the others and he got to the top exhausted and the rest were too impatient and they climbed down without waiting for him and he had to climb down by himself at night when it got cold and he grew up thinking that there was no such thing as loyalty and that friendship was a game for fools and he kept on thinking it until long after the day he died, and he tells you he doesn't offer any of this as an excuse but as an explanation for the crime that sent him to this awful place

and he tells you all of this in an instant

and without thinking you're halfway up the stairs, cradling the machine gun like a baby

and you climb right past First Class to cockpit level, where the bald man is waiting for you, and he tries to kill you as you enter, but he's just candy, and leaping over his body you all but pounce on the microphone hanging from the console and you raise it to your lips and you open your mouth and scream, "Flight Twenty to Tower! Flight Twenty to Tower!"

. . .

and through the speakers a Voice older than Earth and colder than ice says, "This is the Tower," and your knees turn cold and you have to force upon yourself the strength to talk, because that Voice

is the worst you've had to contend with yet; you know Whose voice that is without having to ask; and somehow you manage to shout, "This is Flight Twenty! The Hijacking is Over! Repeat the Hijacking is Over! Request Immediate Clearance to Return to Scheduled Flight Path!"

and the next second and a half is the longest second and half of your life; then the speakers crackle again and the same Voice says, "You may change course as soon as Our prisoner is returned to Us,"

and you say, "We don't have any pilots,"

and the empty eviscerated corpses of the pilots place their cold dead hands on the controls, waiting for further instructions, and their eyes are cold, and alive, and in pain

and the Voice says, "You may change course as soon as Our prisoner is returned to Us,"

and it's clear there will be no negotiation on this issue

. . .

so it's down the stairs again, where the burnt man is standing, with difficulty, at the edge of the furnace. And he is cradling the baby, which looks like it's giving some serious thought toward halting its headlong scream some time soon. And he is crying too. And he looks at the hatchway, and then at you, and then at the hatchway. And you wait for him to make whatever prayers a man already damned may want to make. And then he gives you the baby, leaving hand-shaped soot marks on in its belly, and he turns toward the hatchway, and he stands on the edge of the furnace, and the hot wind lashes at his face, and he turns his back to the fire, and he looks at you, wearing the infinitely sad expression of a man who's atoned for everything way too late

and then he's gone

and you close the hatch

and the baby sobs softly on your shoulder, and the sounds of screams disappear, everywhere outside the plane

and you sit down right where you are, in the aisle, on the carpet and you bow your head in the first prayer you've uttered in years

mourning your wife, and your fellow passengers, and the repentant soul of Judas Iscariot.

The Soft Whisper of Midnight Snow

CHARLES DE LINT

Introduction

A lot of the stories in the Hardback Magazine were dark. Most of Charles de Lint's stories are not, and yet he was in almost every issue. We also published a lot of his work in our Axolotl Press line.

"The Soft Whisper of Midnight Snow" is one of my favorites of his. It's evocative and gentle. Fantasy, particularly fantasy short stories, moved in Charles's direction over the years, but in the early 1990s, his short work wasn't considered mainstream at all.

Over the years, Charles has published more than eighty novels. He is the recipient of the World Fantasy, Aurora (three times), Sunburst, and White Pine awards, among others and was recently inducted into the Canadian SF & Fantasy Association Hall of Fame.

He's also a musician and a poet. That lyricism informs all of his work, just as it does here.

The Soft Whisper of Midnight Snow

Charles de Lint

Night. The fields lay stark as a charcoal drawing—white drifts, the black-clawed talons of the trees, the starlight piercingly bright. A gust of wind-driven snow swirled across the nearest field and he was there again. A shape in the twisting snow. A whisper of moccasins against white grains of ice. One step, another. He was drawing closer, much closer. Then she blinked, the snow swirled with a new flurry of wind, and he was gone. The field lay empty.

Tomilyn Douglas turned from the window and let out a breath she hadn't been aware of holding. The cabin was warm, the new woodstove throwing off all of its advertised heat, but a chill still scurried down her spine. She walked slowly to where her easel stood by an east window, ready to make use of the morning light. Her hand trembled slightly as she flicked a lamp switch and studied the drawing in its pale glow. It twinned the scene she had just been witness to, complete with the tiny shapeless figure, its details hidden in a swirl of gusting snow.

This morning she'd thought it had been a dream, that she had only dreamed of waking and seeing that figure in the snow, moving towards the cabin. Her fingers smudged with charcoal, she'd stood back and smiled with satisfaction at the rendering she'd done of it, that momentary high of a completed work making her a little dizzy until she'd had to go sit down. A useful dream, she'd thought, for it had left her with the first piece of decent work she'd completed since Alan...since Alan had gone. It was an omen of things to come, of a lost talent returned, of an ache finally beginning to heal.

Tomi flicked off the light and the room returned to darkness. It'd been an omen all right, she thought. But she was no longer so sure that she understood just what it was that it promised.

———

"This is where the dream becomes real," he'd told her when they bought and fixed up the cabin. It was meant to be only a temporary arrangement. The cabin stood on a hundred acres of bushland south of Calabogie. Alan had the blueprints all drawn up for the house they would build on the hill behind the cabin. It was his dream to build a home for them that would be the perfect design. The house would grow almost organically from its surroundings. A stand of birch grew so close to where her studio would be that she would feel as though she was a part of the forest, separated only by the glass walls of the room. Solar heating, a vegetable garden already planned out, enough forest on the land that they could cut their own wood... Self-sufficiency was to be the order of the day and she loved him for it. For the house, for the land, for the dream, for...for his love.

They could afford to live out of the city. They were both established in their careers—architect and artist. Alan's clients sought him out now, while her work sold as quickly as she could paint it. They were the perfect match for each other—she loved it when people told them that, because it was true. For eleven years...it was true. But the dream had become a nightmare.

Last spring the foundations of their dream house were a scar on the landscape, like the scar on her soul. The forest began to reclaim its own. By the time the snows came this year, the sharp edges of the foundations were rounded with returning undergrowth. The scar she carried had yet to lose its raw edges.

Morning. Tomi bundled up and went out into the field but if last night's visitor had left any tracks, if he hadn't just been some figment of her imagination, the night's wind had dusted and filled them with snow. She stood, the wind blowing her brown hair into her face, and stared across the white expanse of drifts and dervishing snow eddies to study the forest beyond the fields. The quiet that she'd loved when she moved here from the city, that she'd slowly come to love again as she dealt with her pain, disturbed her now. Too quiet, she thought, then she spoke the clichéd words aloud. The wind took them from her mouth and scattered them across the field. Shivering, Tomi returned to the cabin.

She spent the day working at her easel. Sketch after sketch made its mysterious passage from mind through fingers to paper. And they were all good. No, she amended as she looked them over while having a midafternoon soup-and-tea break. They were better than good. They were the best she'd done in over a year, perhaps better than before Alan—

She shut that train of thought off as quickly as it came. She was getting better at it now. But while she thrust aside the ache before it could take hold, she couldn't shake the uneasiness that had followed her through the day. Night was coming, was almost here. Just at dusk it began to snow. Tiny granular pellets rasped against the door, rattled on the roof. She wanted to turn all the lights on so that she'd be blinded to the night outside, but not seeing made her more nervous. One by one she turned them off, then sat in the darkness and looked out over the fields at the falling snow.

One day he just never came home. She could draw up that day in her memory with a total recall that always struck her as a sure sign that she was still a long way from getting over it. He left in the morning to do some work down the road at Sam Gould's place—Sam having helped them when they were having the foundation poured. When he still wasn't back by dinnertime, she gave Sam a call, but he hadn't seen Alan all day and, no, he hadn't been expecting him.

That night wasn't the worst one in her life—those had come after, when she knew—but it was bad. She hadn't been able to do anything but worry, staring at the phone, waiting for him to call. She tried some friends of theirs in the city. No luck. She thought of calling the police, hospitals, that kind of thing, but knew for all her worry that it was too early for that. Then around eleven o'clock the phone rang, startling her right out of her seat with its klaxon jangle.

"Alan?" she cried into the mouthpiece. "Alan, is that you?" The words came out in a rush like they were all one word.

"Whoa, Mrs. Douglas. Slow down a bit. This is Tom Moulton." Her relief shattered into pieces of icy dread.

"Sorry to be calling you so late, but I was talking to Sam a few minutes ago and heard you were worried about your man. Thing is, I saw your jeep parked out on 511, a couple of miles down from my place. I knew right off it was yours, but I figured you all were out for a little hike or something, you know what I mean?"

She called the police then, and they began a search of the surrounding bush. It wasn't until a couple of days later when she had to go to the bank that she discovered half the money in their joint account had been withdrawn.

Night. The snow had tapered off, but the wind was still shaping and reshaping the drifts around the trees and fence posts and up against the cabin. Tomi was half-hypnotized by the movement of the snow. Time and again she thought she saw a figure, but it was always just a shadow movement, a tree branch, a fox once. Then just as she was ready to give up her vigil, something drew her face closer to the window and she saw him again.

He was closer still. Not moving now, just standing out there in the field, watching the cabin. Tattered cloth fluttered in the wind, muting his outline against the snow. He was still too far away to make out details, but something about the way he stood, about the way he held himself erect, not hunched into the wind, told her that he wasn't who she'd feared he'd be. He wasn't Alan.

"Who are you?" she whispered. "What do you want from me?" She didn't expect an answer. He was too far away to hear her.

There was a thick glass pane and an expanse of white field between them. There was the wind and the gusting snow to steal her words. She wanted to shout at the figure, to run out and grab him. The window frosted up under her breath. She cleared it with a quick wipe of her hand, but in the time it took the figure was gone again.

Hardly realizing what she was doing, she grabbed her coat and a flashlight and ran outside, stumbling through the snow to where he'd stood. When she reached the spot there was no sign of him, no tracks. The field was virgin snow all around her, except for her own ragged trail from the cabin.

She began to shiver. Returning to the warmth of the cabin, she closed and bolted the door. She tossed her coat onto a chair, the flashlight, never used, on top of it, then slowly made her way to her bedroom. She began to undress, then stopped dead as she glanced at the bed. A long raven's feather lay on the comforter, stark and black against its flowered Laura Ashley design.

"Oh, Jesus."

On watery legs she walked over to the bed, stared at the intrusion, unwilling to touch it. He'd been inside. Somehow, while she'd been out looking for him, in those few moments, he'd come inside. Slowly she backed out of the bedroom. It didn't take long to search the cabin. There was the main room that included her studio and the kitchen area, a bathroom, and her bedroom. She was alone in the cabin. In a trancelike state, she investigated every possible hiding place until she was positive of that. She was alone inside, but he was out there. What did he want? What in God's name was this game he was playing? She was a long time getting to sleep that night, starting at every familiar creak and groan of her cabin. When she finally did sleep, restless dreams plagued her, dreams of shapeless figures and clouds of raven's feathers that fell like black snow all around her while she ran and ran, trying to catch an answer that was always out of reach. Underpinning her dreams, the wind moaned outside the cabin, whispering the snow against its log walls.

The deed to the cabin and its land was in her name and, once the initial shock was over, she was quick to remove what money remained in their joint account into one under her own name. She kept thinking there was some mistake, that this wasn't happening to them, to her. But as the days drifted into weeks, she had no choice but to accept it. To believe it, even if she couldn't understand it.

At first she was confused and hurt. Anger was there too, but it came and went as if of its own will. Mostly she felt worthless. If they'd been having fights, if there'd been another woman, if there'd been some hint of what was coming, maybe she could have accepted it more easily. But it had come out of the blue.

"It's him," her friends tried to convince her. "He's just an asshole, Tomi. Christ, he never had it so good."

Neither had she, she'd want to say, but the words never got beyond her thinking them. He'd left her and she knew why. Because she was worthless. As she tried to lose herself in her work during the following weeks, she saw that her art was worthless too. God, no wonder he'd left her. The real wonder was that he hadn't left her sooner.

And even later as she, at least intellectually, came to realize that it *was* him and not her worthlessness that had made him leave, emotionally it wasn't that easy to accept. Emotionally, she retained the feelings of her own inadequacy. She'd stare into a mirror and see her face drawn and pale with her anxiety, the brown hair that framed it hanging listless, the body that could have been exercised but instead had been left to sag.

"Who'd want me?" she'd ask that reflection and then would retire deeper into the shell she was building around herself. Who'd want her? She didn't even want herself.

———

Morning. Tomi had the jeep on the road and was halfway to Ottawa by the time the nine o'clock CBC news came on the radio. She turned it off. Her own troubles were enough to bear without having to listen to the world's. But once she was in Ottawa, she didn't know why she'd come.

She'd had to get away from the cabin, from the figure that haunted the fields outside it, from the black feather that was lying on the floor of her bedroom, but being here didn't help. There was too much going on, too many cars, too many people. She almost had a couple of accidents in the heavy traffic on the Queensway, another on Bank Street.

She'd been planning to visit friends, but no longer knew what to say to them. Running from the cabin wasn't the answer, she realized.

Just as withdrawing from the world after Alan had left hadn't been an answer. She had to go back.

————

That first spring alone had been the worst. She hadn't been able to look at the foundations without wanting to cry. Unable to paint, or even sketch, she'd thrown herself into working around the cabin, fixing it up, removing every trace of Alan from it, putting in a garden, buying a new woodstove, discovering talents she'd never known she'd had. She might not be able to keep a husband or express herself with her art anymore, but she could handle a hammer and saw, she could chop firewood, she could do a lot of things now—do them without ever worrying about whether or not she was capable of them.

The first night that she made a vegetable stew with all the ingredients coming out of her own garden, she celebrated with a bottle of wine, got very drunk, and never once wanted to cry. She stood out in the clear night air and looked up the hill at the foundations and was surprised at what she found in herself.

The ache was still there, but it was different now. Still immediate, but not quite so piercing. She might not be able to paint yet, but the next day she took out her sketchbook and began to draw again. She wasn't happy with anything she did, but she wasn't discouraged about it anymore either. Not in the same way as she'd been when Alan first had deserted her.

————

Night. Tomi had forgotten how quickly it got dark. She decided to return to the cabin, but since she was in town anyway, she thought she might as well make a day of it. It went by all too quickly. From grocery shopping to haunting used bookstores and antique shops, it was going on four o'clock before she knew it. By the time she was fighting the heavy traffic on her way home, it began to snow again, big heavy flakes that were whisked away by the jeep's wipers but were building up rapidly on the road and fields. When she reached old Highway 1 going north from Lanark, she was reduced to a slow crawl, even with the jeep's four-wheel drive. The buildup of snow and ice made for treacherous driving, especially on roads like this without as much traffic.

After Highway 1 turned into 511 and crossed the Clyde River, the driving grew worse. Here the road was narrow and twisted its way through the wooded hills that were barely visible through the storm. The wind drove the snow in sheets across her windshield. The jeep plowed through drifts that had already thrust halfway across the road in places.

Not far now, she told herself, and that much was true, but a half mile from the laneway leading in to her cabin, the road took a sudden dip and a sharp turn at the same time. She was going too fast when she topped the hill and hit an icy patch. Already nervous, she did the worst thing possible and instead of riding the fishtail and easing out of it, she slammed her foot on the brake.

The jeep skidded, came sideways down the hill and missed the turn. Its momentum took it through and then over the snow embankment until it thudded to a stop against a tall pine. The shock of the impact brought all the snow down from its branches in a sudden avalanche. Panicked and shaken, Tomi snapped loose her seatbelt and lunged from the jeep. The snow came up to her hips as she floundered through it back to the road. She was breathing heavily by the time she reached it, the cold air hurting her lungs. When she looked back, she saw the jeep was half-covered with the snow that it had dislodged from the pine.

She was never going to get it out of that mess. Not without a tow truck or tractor. But she couldn't face seeing to that now. She wasn't far from home. She could walk the half mile easily. Trying to ignore the chill that was seeping in through her clothes, cold enough to make even her bones feel cold, she forced her way back to the jeep, fetched her purse and groceries, and started the short trek home.

The snow was coming down in a fury now, the wind slapping it against her exposed skin with enough force to hurt. Neck hunched into her coat, head bowed, she trudged up the road, fighting the steadily growing drifts. The half mile had never seemed so long. Her boots—fine for town, but a joke out here—were wet and cold against her feet. The stylish three-quarter length coat that was only meant for the quick dashes from warm vehicle to warm store couldn't contend with the bone-piercing chill of the wind.

She got a scare when she stumbled and fell in a sprawl on the highway, her grocery bag splitting open to spew its contents all around her. But she was more scared when she found she just couldn't get up to go on. The shock of the accident and the numbing cold had drained all her strength.

She could lie here and, with the poor visibility, the snowplow would come by and bury her in the embankment, never knowing that its blades had scooped her up and shunted her aside. Or a pickup could come by and run her down before its driver even realized what it was that he was about to hit.

Right, bright eyes, she thought. So get the hell out of here.

She managed to sit up and tried to scrape together her scattered groceries, but her fingers were too numb in their thin gloves to work properly. What a time to play fashion horse, she thought hazily. But then again she hadn't been planning on playing the arctic explorer when she'd set out this morning. What a dramatic picture this would make, she decided. The woman fallen in the snow, her groceries scattered around her, the wind howling around her like a dervish....

She blinked her eyes open suddenly to find that she'd laid her head down on the road again as she'd been thinking. This. Wouldn't. Do. She forced herself back up into a sitting position.

Screw the groceries. If she didn't get out of here quickly, she wasn't going to get up at all.

But the cold was in her bones now. Her teeth chattered and her jaws ached from trying to keep them from doing so. Her hands and feet just felt like lumps on the ends of the arms and legs. She realized with a shock that she was almost completely covered with snow. Only her upper torso was relatively free, the snow covering it having fallen off when she sat up.

Up. That was the ticket. She had to get up, put one foot in front of the other, and get herself home. She tried to rise, but the cold had just sapped something in her. There's been a lot of times over the past spring and summer when she'd simply wanted to die, but now that it was a very real possibility, she wanted to live with a fierceness that actually got her to her feet.

She tottered and took a couple of steps, then fell into another drift, frustrated tears freezing on her cheeks. Which was weird, she thought, because the snow actually felt warm now. It was cozy. Just like her bed in the cabin. Or the big easy chair in front of the woodstove...

As she began to drift off, the last thing she saw was a dark shape moving towards her through the billowing snow. Incongruously, for all the howling of the wind, she heard a rasp of bead and quill against leather, a whisper of moccasins against the crust of the snow, smelled a pungent scent like a freshly snapped cedar bough, and then she knew no more.

————

She blinked awake. The air was thickly warm around her. She was lying on something soft, cozily wrapped in a coverage of furs. Dim lighting spun in her gaze as she sat up. When her head stopped spinning, she stared groggily about herself.

There was a fire crackling in front of her, its smoke escaping upward through a hole in the roof. Roof. Where was she? The walls looked like they were made of woven branches. She could hear the wind howling outside them. Movement caught her eye and she looked across the fire. He'd been sitting so still that she hadn't noticed him at first, but now he leapt out at her with a thousand details, each one so clear that she wondered how she could have taken so long to see him there.

He sat cross-legged on a deerskin, the firelight playing on his pale skin, waking sharp highlights in his narrow features. His clothing was a motley collection of tatters. A black shirt, decorated with bone. A grey vest, inlaid with beadwork, quills, and feathers. A raven's skull hung like a pendent from his neck in the middle of a cluster of feathers and shells. He wore a headdress, again decorated with feathers and bones, that lifted high above his head in the shape of a pair of horns. She thought of the wicked queen in Disney's *Sleeping Beauty*, looking at those horns, or of Tolkien's highborn elves, taking in his pale features. But there was more of the Native American about him. And more than that, a feeling of great sorrow.

"Who...who are you?" she asked. She spoke softly, the way one might speak to a wild animal, poised for flight. "Why were you watching my cabin? What do you want with me?" She knew it had to have been him.

He made no reply. His eyes seemed all white in the deceptive light cast by the fire, all except for their pale gray pupils. His gaze never left Tomi's face. She was suddenly sure that she was dead. The plow *had* come by and scraped her frozen body up from the road, burying it under a mountain of snow. He was here to take her to...to wherever you went when you died.

"Please," she said, fingers tightening their grip on the fur covering. "What...what do you want with me?"

The silence stretched until Tomi thought she would scream. She plucked nervously at the furs, wanting to look away, but her gaze seemed to be trapped by his unblinking eyes.

"Please," she began again. "Why have you been spying on me?"

He nodded suddenly. Movement made the bones and quills

click against each other. "Life," he said. His voice was husky and rough. He spoke with a heavy accent so that Tomi knew that whatever his native language was, it wasn't English.

She swallowed thickly. Fear made her throat dry and tight. "Llife?" she managed. She looked for the door of the lodge, trying not to be too obvious about it. She didn't know if she'd have the strength to take off, but she couldn't just stay here with…with whatever he was.

He pulled a strip of birchbark from under his tunic and took a charred twig from beside the fire. With quick deft movements, he began to sketch on the birchbark. Curiosity warred with fear inside Tomi and she leaned forward. When he suddenly thrust the finished drawing at her, she floundered to get out of the way, then chided herself. So far the stranger hadn't hurt her. He'd brought her in from the cold and snow, bundled her up in his furs, saved her life….

And the drawing…it was good. Better than good.

Tomi taught art from time to time, week-long courses at the Haliburton School during the summer, a few at Algonquin College in Ottawa. Not one of those students' work could hold a candle to the lifelike sketch of a snow hare that her curious host had thrust at her. His quick deft rendering of it was what she always tried to instill in her students. To go for feeling first. She smiled to show she appreciated it.

"It's very good," she began.

"Life!" he repeated. Taking back the drawing, he blew on it, then laid it on the ground beside the fire.

Fear clawed up Tomi's spine again as the lines of the drawing began to move, to lift three-dimensionally from the birchbark. A hazily shaped hare sat there, its outline smoky and indistinct. Nose twitching nervously, it regarded her with warm eyes. Her fear died, replaced with wonder. She reached out a hand to touch the little apparition, but it drifted apart like smoke and was gone. All that remained was the birchbark that it had been sitting on. Its surface was clear, unmarked. "You," her host said. "*Your* breath."

"I...I can't breathe like...like..."

"You must."

"I can't breathe—" Suddenly the lodge was spinning again. The fire turned into a whirlpool of glittering sparks, that twisted and danced like snow-driven wind. Tomi's words froze in her throat. Gone. It was going. It was—

———

—gone.

"—can't breathe...."

Something was shaking her. She blinked rapidly, trying to slow down the spinning.

"Miz Douglas? Miz Douglas?"

The world came into focus with a sharp snap. A face was leaning into hers. For one moment, she was back in the storm, or the storm had torn apart the strange man's lodge, blowing everything away, then she recognized the face. Sam Gould's strong features were looking down into hers. Worry creased his face. He looked at a loss.

"Sam...?"

"It's me, Miz Douglas. Found you lying on the highway. You're damned lucky I didn't run over you with the plow, I'll tell you that."

"You...found me...?" Then the lodge, the man—that had been a dream?

"Sure did. Funny thing—thought I saw someone standing beside you, just when my high beams picked you out, but that must've been you standing for a moment, just before you fell. Hell of a storm, though, and that's fact. Had a look at your jeep, but it's in too deep for me to do much about it till the morning. I'll come round with the tractor then, if you can wait."

"I...I can wait."

"Not much damage, considering. Headlight's gone on the driver's side. You might want Bill Cassidy to have a look at that fender. I figure he could straighten her out for you, no problem."

"There was… someone standing…?" Tomi managed.

"Well, I thought there was, I'll tell you that. But it was just a trick of the lights, I'd say. Storm can fool you into thinking you're seeing just about anything sometimes."

"Yes," Tomi said slowly. Like what she'd thought she'd seen. A dream. Just….

"Anyway, I brought you up to your cabin," Sam continued. "Thought you might'a had a touch of frostbite on your wrist there, but I wrapped it up tight and kept it warm. The skin wasn't broken, so it'll be all right. You were lucky, and that's fact. I coulda plowed you right up into the bank and no one would've known to go looking for you till your jeep was spotted in the morning. I put you to bed, but 'cepting your boots and coat, I didn't…you know…" He blushed. "I just covered you up, Miz Douglas."

"Thank you, Sam." Tomi sat up slowly. "You saved my life." A dream?

Sam shuffled his feet. "Guess I did at that. I woulda called up an ambulance, but by the time it would've got here, well…I did what I could, I'll tell you that. You want I should call up the doc now, Miz Douglas? Or maybe get someone to stay with you for the night?"

Tomi shook her head. "I'll be all right, Sam. But thank you." Just a dream?

"My pleasure. I'd best be going now. Weather's not getting any better and I've got a load of plowing still to do. Keep me busy most of the night, I'll tell you that."

Tomi started to get up, but Sam laid a hand on her shoulder and gently pressed her down. "I can see myself out, Miz Douglas. You just lie there and take her easy. I'll lock up and be back in the morning with the tractor. You just get some sleep now. You've been through a rough time, and that's a fact. Sleep's the best thing for you now."

Tomi nodded and lay back, knowing that he wouldn't go until she did. She listened to him clomp across the hardwood floors in his work boots, heard him tug on his parka, the sound of the zipper, the door opening. "I'll see you in the morning!" he called, then the door slammed shut. The door handle made a click-click noise as he checked to make sure it was locked. Silence then for a time. Except for the wind. The snow being pushed against the cabin, the windows. The big snow plow starting up. Gears grinding as they changed. The truck backing out of her lane. Silence again as the sound of the engine was swallowed by the wind.

Tomi stared at her ceiling. Just a dream?

She listened to the wind and the whisper of the snow against the window panes and logs outside. She might have drifted off, she wasn't sure, just dozed there, until suddenly she had to get up, had to see, *had* to. She padded out of her bedroom into the main room of the cabin. Sam had left the lights on and she turned them off, one by one, then went to stand by the window.

The snow was still falling, the wind blowing it in great sweeps across the field. She stared out at the field, willing her stranger to be there again, for it not to have been a dream. She wasn't sure what she wanted, what she expected. She had been frightened in the lodge, but remembering it now, there had been no reason for fear. Just the strange man with his totemic clothing, and the drawing that came to life with a breath, with just a whisper of air drawn up from his lungs....

She moved to her easel and turned on a light, aiming it so that it pooled over the easel, leaving the rest of the room in shadows. From the closet, she took out a virgin canvas, a sketching pencil, her acrylics. The sketching went easily. Background first, light, hazy as though seen through a gossamer curtain of falling snow. Then the figure. But close now.

She knew his features and quickly sketched them in. Left

their look of sorrow, but imbued them with a certain air of nobility as well. She made the clothing not so ragged, not so tattered. The totemic raven skulls, feathers, beads and quills, came readily, leaping the gap from memory to canvas with an exhilarating ease.

Oh, lord. This was what it felt like. This was what she'd missed, what Alan had stolen from her, what the stranger had given her back. She didn't know who or what he was, realized that it didn't matter.

Dream or real, it didn't matter. Some spirit of winter, of the snow and wind, or of the forest or a creation of her own blocked creativity.

It didn't matter.

When the sketching was filled in as much as she needed, she moved straight to the acrylics, mixing the paints and applying them, scarcely paying any attention to what she was doing. Her subconscious remembered, her fingers remembered. She only had to give them free rein. She only had to breathe life into what took shape on her canvas. God. To have forgotten this…to have lost it….

She leaned close as she worked, mixing colors on the seat of the stool, too enrapt in her work to search for her palette. The shades came easily. The painting grew from the rough black and white sketch into a being almost composed of flesh and blood, almost as though she was back in his lodge, seeing him across the fire, the light playing on his features, his steady gaze never wavering from hers. She listened to the wind, to the hiss and spit of the snow against the windows, and smiled as she worked.

———

It was long after midnight, but still far from dawn, when the main figure was completed and she only had the background to fill in. Her gaze locked to the gaze of the figure in the painting as she brushed in the pines and cedars behind him, the swirl of the snow as it gusted through the trees, across the field. But for all the movement in the background, the figure in the foreground was still. Only his eyes spoke to her.

Her fingers were cramping when she heard, under the moan of the wind and the whisper of the snow, the sound of her locked door opening. A draft of cold air touched the back of her neck as the wind entered, the wind and something more, something she had no name for, but she knew she owed it a debt.

It didn't matter what he was—her imagination running wild, or something out of the wild night sparking her imagination. She was repaying what he had recovered for her from that first moment she'd seen him in the field, just a dark shape in the blurring snow, repaying what had been lost and now regained with life.

The door closed, but she didn't turn around. The painting in front of her was like a mirror and she continued to breathe on it as she finished the last cedar.

Offerings

SUSAN PALWICK

Introduction

I'm not sure why, but Susan Palwick's "Offerings" is a short story that I think about often, especially when my house is just a tad dirty and the cats are just a little bit cranky.

Unlike some of the other writers in this volume, Susan doesn't write enough for my tastes. A former English professor, she's now busy doing difficult and important work as a hospital chaplain and lay preacher.

Offerings

Susan Palwick

"The little people feed on anything that's evil," Matthew's mother told him when he was very young. "They're like the spiders in the garden, Matthew, which look ugly but are really good, because they eat the bugs which kill the flowers."

Matthew didn't like spiders, and he didn't like Mother's description of the little people, who smelled like old leaves and had small teeth as sharp as razors. "They really aren't that different from Nutmeg," Mother always said, but she made Matthew bathe the dog once a week and screamed whenever she found another dead squirrel in the kitchen, so he guessed that she wasn't as fond of smells and teeth as she claimed. Nutmeg redeemed herself by fetching sticks and sleeping in a warm heap at the foot of Matthew's bed every night, but he knew from his mother's stories that the little people were neither playful nor comforting.

"They saved your grandfather's life," she told Matthew. She'd tell him the story when he was helping her bake cookies in the kitchen, or when she was knitting sweaters for him to wear to school, or on wet days when he couldn't play outside. "It was when I was a little girl. He used to drink all the time and he'd turned bad, oh so bad, Matthew. He was running around with other women, and one night my mother tried to kick him out and he broke all her best dishes, the set from England that was decorated with real gold leaf—just took them down off the shelves and started smashing them on the floor. She tried to stop him and he hit her, and then he tried to hit me too but she got between us. She was a big woman. So she hit *him* and he fell and knocked his head against the table—maybe he passed out then, I don't know, but anyhow she dragged him outside and left him there and locked the door. It was raining. I made her go back out and turn him on his side instead of on his back, so he wouldn't drown from the water running in his nose...oh, I was scared. I thought he was going to die, and Mother kept saying, 'Your real daddy died a long time ago; your real daddy was loving and faithful and didn't break things. The whiskey killed him, Miriam. Don't cry for that mean drunk out there.'

"But I did anyway. I went to bed and cried myself to sleep, and in the middle of the night I woke up because he'd started screaming, out there in the rain. He kept screaming, 'Go away, go away! Stop hurting me!' I ran into my mother's room and got under the covers with her, and she said, 'Don't be scared. Nobody's hurting him but his own demons,' and finally we heard him say, 'All right, all right, I'll stop, I promise,' and then he stopped screaming. Mother got up and let him back in—oh, he was scared, white as a sheet and shaking like a leaf. He told us how the little people had come up to him in the dark and bitten him, bitten him all over with their sharp little teeth. There were too many of them to count, he said; they gnawed at his fingers and toes and nibbled on his legs and chewed on his nose, and they drank his blood the way he drank whiskey. He knew he was going to die and he promised that if they didn't kill him he'd stop drinking and fooling around and hitting us—and the minute he said that all the wounds healed up like they'd never been there at all, and all the little people went away, because he wasn't evil anymore. And he kept that promise, too: he never touched a drop after that, and he got a good job and bought my mother new dishes and never looked at anybody else. He was a wonderful man after that, loving and faithful just like my mother had said, and whenever anybody asked him what had made him change he said, 'It was the little people. I thought they were going to kill me, but they really saved my life.'"

Matthew was fascinated by the story; Matthew's father hated it. "It's crazy nonsense, Miriam! Matthew, your grandfather was having DTs and seeing things, that's all. That's why the bite marks healed up like they'd never been there: they hadn't! You've never seen one of these critters, have you?"

"Have you ever seen a germ?" his mother countered. "No, of course not. But they still make you sick, just like the little people made my father well."

Germs smelled like Listerine and the little people smelled like dead leaves. These invisibilities were every bit as real to Matthew as Mother herself, who smelled like warm cookies, or Miss Summersong at school, who smelled like lavender and gave him special books to read, or Daddy, who smelled like gin.

As Matthew grew taller Nutmeg became progressively better at killing squirrels, and the books Miss Summersong gave Matthew became more difficult. Daddy smelled like gin more and more often, and Mother like cookies less and less. They fought in the evenings when Matthew was supposed to be sleeping, as he lay in bed with Nutmeg curled heavily on his feet, chasing squirrels in her sleep; to escape the words Mother and Daddy hurled at each other Matthew thought about Miss Summersong's books, some of which were about magical kingdoms and some of which were about science.

Matthew believed as completely in both as he still did in the little people. He knew from the rustlings and scamperings he heard at night that they lived in the woods just beyond the house; sometimes, during a lull in his parents' fighting, he heard soft chewing noises outside and imagined the little people feasting on evil, but he could no longer tell if they were a protection or a threat.

"Squirrels," Daddy said once when Matthew described the noises, but it couldn't be squirrels. Nutmeg, who could hear a squirrel from three miles away through a thunderstorm, always slept soundly through these disturbances.

"You see?" Mother said. "Nutmeg isn't scared of them and neither should you be, Matthew. Your father, on the other hand—"

"Raccoons," Daddy said, refilling his orange juice glass with gin. "Muskrats. Maybe a bunch of bunny rabbits are having an orgy and the dog isn't interested because their tails aren't long enough, okay? Jesus, Miriam! You'll have the kid believing in flying saucers if you keep this up."

"You're disgusting," she said. "Eat some breakfast like a decent—"

"I'm not decent and I don't want breakfast; I want a drink."

"I hope they come and nibble you bare as a corncob and take all your bottles—"

"And do what? Pour them down the sink the way you do? Hey, Matt, the little critters actually live in the plumbing, didja know that? Your mother's been treating them to a party every night, or else she likes 'em a lot less than she says she does and she's trying to drown them. But it doesn't matter. There's enough for all of us. Here, kid—try some."

Matthew's mother started screaming at Daddy then, but Daddy only laughed. "I'd better go wait for the bus," Matthew said, ignoring the proffered glass and giving his last piece of bacon to Nutmeg. His stomach ached, as it always did at breakfast. He knew he'd feel better as soon as he got on the school bus.

One morning when Matthew was ten the bus didn't come. There had been a heavy snowstorm the night before, and when Matthew had been waiting in front of the house for an hour, Mother came to fetch him back inside.

"The bus isn't coming, Matthew; they just said so on the radio. The roads are too bad. There won't be any school today."

Matthew followed her into the house along the narrow path he'd shoveled for himself earlier that morning. Daddy sat in the kitchen, his hands clenched around a mug which held nothing but coffee. Mother must have emptied his bottles the night before, although Matthew wasn't sure when she'd had time. The fighting from his parents' bedroom had gone on until dawn, long past Matthew's ability to block it out by thinking about schoolwork. He hadn't even been able to hear the little people over the din.

"Look what you're doing to Matthew," Mother had yelled, and Daddy had answered just as loudly, "Matthew's fine, nothing's wrong with him, what's Matthew got to do with it anyway?"

"I want to go to school," Matthew told them, his stomach clenching. He didn't want to have anything to do with it. He wanted to be with Miss Summersong with her silver braided hair, Miss Summersong who had been giving him books since he was five, who could make him forget about the drinking and the fighting and living in the woods so far from everyone else. "Why can't I go to school?"

"Because of the roads," Mother said.

Daddy let go of the coffee mug and pressed his hands flat on the table to keep them from shaking. It didn't work. "Matthew, if you really want to go I'll drive you. Get in the truck."

"No! You're in no shape to drive, or the truck to be driven, or the roads to be driven on. The school's probably closed, anyway. Matthew, take your coat off."

Daddy clenched his hands into fists and jammed them into his pockets. "The radio said it was open. You heard it, Miriam."

"Well, I'm sure Miss Summersong won't be there."

"Miss Summersong's always there," Matthew told her.

"Matthew, he doesn't really want to take you to school! He's just looking for an excuse to go to town and buy more liquor. Don't you understand?"

He understood, but he didn't care. His father would go to

town anyway, and if anything was moving toward the school-house Matthew wanted to be in it. The truck was aged and rusting, the roads nearly impassible; Daddy cursed and clutched the steering wheel while Matthew prayed and clutched his books. He prayed to Miss Summersong and to the little people, both of whom were much closer than God.

His prayer to Miss Summersong was simple: please be there. He asked more complex things of the little people, things he knew they probably couldn't grant, things he didn't know if they'd be able to understand because he wasn't sure he understood them himself. Please don't say I'm evil, he prayed, please don't call me evil for wanting to go to school and giving Daddy an excuse to go to town, please stay outside the house, please leave me alone and leave Mother and Daddy alone too, don't eat us, I don't want to be eaten and I don't want them to be eaten because then where would I live? I'll give you anything you want, but leave the three of us alone.

He prayed all the way to school, but he didn't know if his supplications were appeasing the little people or only catching their attention. As Matthew walked into the schoolroom that morning it seemed as if the little people must be very close and very hungry, and not even the sight of Miss Summersong waiting for him, smiling because he was the only one of her fifteen students who'd managed the trip through the snow, could make him feel less afraid.

"I won't give you regular work today, Matthew, because the other children aren't here. We'll just do special things." So they talked about the books she'd given him, about the Arabian Nights and Oz and the biology book which had pictures of a man's body stripped of its skin, of its muscles, finally even of its organs, so that just the bones were left; they talked about rocks and stars and animals, but through all of it Matthew kept thinking about Daddy driving in the snowstorm and the little people in the woods. Finally Miss Summersong said, "Matthew, what's the matter? You seem unhappy today."

"Nothing's the matter," Matthew told her. It was too compli-
cated, and if he told her what had happened she might be angry
at him for coming to school at all. He wondered if she could tell
he was lying. But she only sighed and said, "I have something to
show you—I'd meant to save it until the others were here too,
but I think maybe today would be a good day for it. Wait here."

She went to the closet at the back of the room and came
back with a microscope. Matthew had only seen microscopes in
books, being used in clean, orderly rooms by people who wore
white coats and wise expressions. Microscopes were as foreign
and incomprehensible as banks and satellites, and it had never
occurred to Matthew that *he* might one day be allowed to handle
such a thing.

The slides Miss Summersong showed him, of bits of flowers
and seeds like battleships under the lens and tiny insects' eyes
grown into faceted jewels, managed to make him forget about
the snow and his parents for a little while. He looked at a speck
of dust and saw a mountain; he examined a downy feather and
saw filaments as rough and gigantic as a monster's tentacles. But
as he was putting away the most beautiful slide, a fragment of
butterfly wing as intricate as some distant city, it slipped from his
hand the same way the road had slid under the wheels of the
truck, and shattered to shards on the schoolroom floor.

Matthew cried out and bent to retrieve the pieces, but they
were too small; even had he been able to gather them all up
again he never would have been able to reassemble them. "I'm
sorry, Miss Summersong, I'm so sorry, I didn't mean to do it,
really I didn't—"

She frowned at him and said, "Of course you didn't,
Matthew. It's all right. We'll clean it up."

He watched her sweep up the bits of glass with a broom and
dustpan and pour them into the trashcan, and he knew he never
should have been allowed to touch the microscope at all. She
was still frowning and the windows rattled as if someone were
trying to get in, and for a moment Matthew heard the soft, wet

noises of the little people licking their lips. "I'll do extra home-work if you want me to, Miss Summersong. I'll pay for it—"

"It was an accident, Matthew. You don't have to do anything." Her frown deepened, and Matthew stared at the floor, wondering if she'd stop giving him books, now that she knew he couldn't be trusted with anything. But she only said, very gently, "Matthew, look at me. Do you like yourself?"

He stared at her, bewildered. He could easily have answered questions about fractions or muscles or flying carpets, but this one defeated him. Miss Summersong watched him steadily, as if he were a slide under the microscope. He didn't know what she wanted him to say. If it hadn't been for the storm and the little people in the woods, he'd have turned and run outside.

His father's horn honked from the road, and for once Matthew welcomed the sound. "I have to go now, Miss Summersong."

"Saved," she said, and Matthew wondered why she sounded sad. "Well, Matthew, I guess I'll see you tomorrow."

"Are you going to give me any homework?"

She looked thoughtful for a moment. "Yes—yes, I am. Tomorrow morning I want you to tell me three things you like about yourself."

He blinked at her, feeling lost. "That's my homework? No reading?"

"No reading. Reading's gotten too easy for you. My job's to challenge you, Matthew." She smiled then, but she didn't look happy.

The trip home was worse than the trip to school had been. The minute Matthew got into the truck he knew that Daddy hadn't gone home at all, but instead had spent the entire day in town drinking gin. The inside of the car reeked of it; a half empty bottle sloshed on the dashboard, and a full case slid in the back of the truck. "Stocked up," said his father, remarkably coherent. "Got lots this time. She'll never find it all. Did you have a good time al school?"

"I broke a butterfly slide," Matthew said.

"Yeah? So? Have some gin, kid. You'll feel better."

"No. I don't want to." That was the money for groceries, he thought. For milk and bacon and dog food. They won't do anything but fight once we get home, and there won't be anything to eat for dinner, and Mother will blame it all on me because I wanted to go to school.

His mother met them at the door, crying as he had known she would be. "Matthew—Matthew, sweetheart, come inside—"

"What about me, Miriam? Do I get to come inside too?"

"Do whatever you want," she said, tugging Matthew into the house, and he knew that something was very wrong. Something terrible must have happened, for her not to start screaming because Daddy was drunk.

"Matthew," she said, "sweetheart, I'm afraid—"

"Where's Nutmeg?" The dog always threw herself on Matthew the minute he got home. The house felt empty, and too quiet. "What happened to Nutmeg?"

"I—" His mother twisted her hands and turned away from him.

"She—this afternoon she started barking the way she does when there's a squirrel, you know. I didn't want to let her out because of the snow but she kept barking and scratching at the door, so finally I did and off she runs into the woods and—"

"Oh Christ," Daddy said. "Is that all? The dog isn't back yet and it's a national calamity? What's for dinner?"

"Leftovers. You spent the grocery money on liquor; do you think I don't know you by now? Matthew, I went out and called her and I even looked for her in the woods, but she didn't come back—"

"It was the little people," Matthew said, remembering his prayer on the way to school. I'll give you anything you want, but leave the three of us alone. "The little people took her." Three, he'd prayed, three and not four: he should have said four. How could he have forgotten about Nutmeg? And now she was gone, vanished into the snow, made into a meal for horrible creatures with teeth sharper than hers.

"Nobody took her," Daddy said. "She ran off after a squirrel, that's all. She'll be back. Everybody calm down."

Matthew shook his head. "If she's not back by now she's not coming. She never stays out so long. She's dead. They ate her—"

"Matthew, it was a squirrel! A squirrel, all right? You heard what your mother said, how she was barking and all. Aren't you the one who says she doesn't bark at these pixies? She ran outside after something real, and she'll come back when she's caught it. Let's eat dinner!"

"I can't eat," Matthew said. "I feel sick."

His mother knelt beside him and felt his forehead. "Matthew, why would the little people—"

"There aren't any little people! Miriam, can't you see what these stories have—"

"Shut up! Matthew, why would they take Nutmeg?"

Because he had promised her to them without knowing it; but if he told Mother that he'd have to tell her about his prayer, how terrified he was that everyone in the house would be eaten for being evil, how he lay awake at night listening to the fighting. Even if he'd been able to tell his mother that he thought she was evil, he'd have been too ashamed to admit that he'd forgotten Nutmeg in his prayers.

So he lied. "She—she pooped in my bed the other night and I cleaned it up but maybe the little people took her because she was bad—"

"No," his mother said gently. "Matthew, she's a good dog. Having an accident doesn't make you evil, and the little people only eat evil things, harmful things. That's why your grandfather was such a good man after—"

"Miriam, cut it out! Stop feeding him this garbage and feed me some supper."

"No! Why should I? You should have bought food and you

didn't. You bought liquor instead—fine, so make that your dinner! I don't care anymore! They should come for you, the little ones should—oh, you'd make a lovely meal for them!"

Matthew clutched at her hand. She was undoing his prayer of safekeeping, inviting the little people into the house to feed on Daddy, and if that happened Nutmeg would have died for nothing. Daddy hated them so much he wouldn't believe in them even if he saw them. He'd think he was just imagining things even when they were devouring him, and he'd die too. "Mother, stop it! Don't say that. The little people will hear you—"

"Matthew," Daddy said, very quiet now, "there's no one to hear her. The little people don't exist; that's just a scare story... let's fix those leftovers, eh? Nutmeg's playing in the snow. She'll be back soon."

But he was wrong. As anxiously as Matthew waited through the evening, Nutmeg didn't come back. The little people came instead, to claim the meal Mother had promised them.

———

Matthew awoke to find his room perfectly illuminated with moonlight reflected from the snow outside. "It's sunlight, Matthew," Miss Summersong had said that day, "all light is sunlight, moonlight too, which stops somewhere else on its way from the sun before it reaches us"; but whatever heat this light had taken from the sun had been lost long ago. The room was icy in a draft from the hall, and the blankets on Matthew's bed did nothing to warm him without the familiar weight on his feet. He got up, shivering, to close whatever window had been left open.

Halfway down the hall to his parents' room he began to smell a stench of rotting leaves and dead things far too vile to belong to Nutmeg. The bedroom door was open, and Matthew saw the little people climbing in through the open window which was causing the draft.

They crept in one by one, as silent as cats, to gather around the bed where Matthew's parents slept, oblivious, his father unconscious from gin and his mother from despair. They looked incredibly old, those little ones, standing no higher than Matthew's knee and dressed in tattered clothing woven from moss and twigs and bits of shredded fabric they must have found in the woods. Their faces were as wrinkled as raisins around gleaming eyes and teeth which shone like needles in the moonlight. And they were thin: skeleton-gaunt, bones like twigs poking through their decaying garments. For all the times Matthew had heard them feasting, they looked as if they'd starved for centuries.

Nearly gagging from the smell, Matthew crouched in the hallway just outside the door. He was too afraid of drawing attention to himself to call out, "He's not evil, not always, some things about him are good!" How could he explain to the little people how parts of his father could be loving and other parts so horrible, when he couldn't understand it himself?

They kept climbing in the window; it looked as if there were hundreds of them now, swarming around the bed, clambering onto each other's shoulders. Matthew imagined them taking Daddy apart like the man in the biology book, stripping away first the skin and then the muscles and organs, until they found the part of him that was evil. Maybe they only wanted his liver; Miss Summersong said that the liver took poisons out of the blood, and the doctor that Daddy's liver was swollen. Matthew remembered, too, a fairy tale about a witch who stole people's livers to make magic with. But even if the little people only took Daddy's liver, he'd still be dead. Could Matthew somehow convince them to take something which could grow back—a strand of hair, a fingernail, a cell?

And then he remembered the biology book again, which told him that he'd grown from two cells, one from each of his parents, and he knew those cells must have been bad ones. Daddy was evil for drinking and Mother was evil for summoning the little people, but Matthew had helped his father get out of the house to buy liquor, and he'd called the little people before Mother had. He'd prayed that they wouldn't think he was evil, but even the prayer had only proven how bad he was, because he'd forgotten to include Nutmeg. The little people didn't want Daddy at all: Matthew was the one they'd come for.

He turned to run, knowing he was not only wicked but a coward, and the little people saw him at last and scampered to surround him before he could move. They began making a low, horrible sound, a cross between a chuckle and an idling motor, as their eyes and teeth caught glints of moonlight. The smell was unbearable. As they crowded closer Matthew tried frantically to think of some charm or spell, some magic which would drive them away, but all he could remember was his homework assignment.

"Tell me three things you like about yourself," Miss Summersong had said. Three was a number which could make powerful magic, according to any story Matthew had ever read; perhaps Miss Summersong, who knew everything else, had known that the little people would come, and had given him that odd riddle as a weapon against them.

"I like myself because Miss Summersong thinks I'm smart," Matthew whispered as the little people pressed against him. Their eyes brightened, and the chuckling grew louder.

"I like myself because I took good care of Nutmeg and didn't mean to hurt her," Matthew said desperately, shrinking away from them and thinking as hard as he could of the smell of lavender. Accidents weren't evil, Mother had said, and he'd left Nutmeg out of his prayer by accident. He'd been thinking too hard about his parents, but that couldn't be evil, could it? Could trying to protect people be evil?

One more and he might be safe, if the magic worked, if it were strong enough—what, what? He squeezed his eyes shut, trembling, certain he'd feel those teeth tearing into his flesh at any moment, and cried, "I like myself because I love Mother and Daddy!"

There was a gust of wind and stabbing cold. When he opened his eyes the little people were gone, having taken their stench and their uncanny laughter with them. In the pool of moonlight which bathed his parents' bed Mother muttered something in a dream, and Daddy began snoring very softly.

———

It was years before he understood what had happened. Nothing changed after that night. His father kept drinking and his mother kept nagging; the fights were as loud as ever, and Miss Summersong's books even more alluring. Nutmeg never came back, and Matthew never saw the little people again. In time, he came to believe that their visit had been nothing but a nightmare inspired by his mother's vivid, gruesome stories.

He moved away to go to college, and never moved back. He studied biology and chemistry and chose a career in research, becoming one of the wise, solitary men in white coats he had admired so as a child. He traveled to many cities and never ceased finding them beautiful and comforting; wilderness unnerved him, although he could not have said why. Nor could he have explained fully why he neither prayed nor drank, why he handled lab equipment with a care considered extraordinary even by his colleagues, why he married a woman whom he had first noticed because she smelled like lavender.

He was successful in his work and happy in his marriage. He and Molly bought a spacious house in a suburb luxurious with lawns and swimming pools, and had a daughter who grew livelier and more inquisitive with each passing year. He gave Katie the books he had loved as a child, but he wasn't displeased when she spent more time ice-skating and playing softball than doing homework. Her ability to make friends awed him. Because his daughter's childhood was happier than his own, he believed himself safe.

When Katie was sixteen she began coming home from parties later than she should have, her eyes glassy and her breath smelling of beer. Molly talked to her, gently; Matthew tried to be gentle, and failed. When Katie's grades slipped he screamed at her, and saw her withdrawing from him. When she began stealing small amounts of money he retaliated by searching her room; preoccupied with his daughter, he became careless at work. He dropped a culture dish on the lab floor one day, and couldn't understand why it took him an hour to stop shaking.

One Saturday afternoon in May when Katie had stormed out of the house, hurling curses over her shoulder, Matthew went on another search and destroy mission. He found two cans of beer stashed inside Katie's winter boots and carried them, as if they were live grenades, to the kitchen sink. His stomach clenched at the noise the liquid made running into the drain.

"No," he heard behind him, and turned to find Molly standing in the kitchen doorway. "Matthew, that won't work. She's just out buying more; you know she is. Or getting someone to buy it for her." She took a few steps closer and put a hand on his arm. "Matthew—you're doing what your mother did. You know it didn't do any good. Don't you remember?"

He pulled away from her; he didn't want to remember. For a brief, bitter moment he regretted having ever described his parents to his wife. When he spoke, his own voice sounded foreign to him. "What should I do, then?"

"Talk to me," Molly said, and he noticed for the first time how dark the circles had grown under her eyes. "You never talk anymore. Here: come here. Sit down."

She led him to the kitchen table as if he were blind. "You're scared," she said. "I'm scared. Your father died from drinking and now Katie's doing it and you can't save her any more than you could save him, and it isn't fair. But destroying yourself won't change anything. I love you as much as I love her,

Matthew, and I don't know which of you is harder to live with anymore. Do you understand?"

"Don't lecture me," he said, and it was that stranger with the hoarse voice talking again, not himself at all. "I don't know what we did wrong, but I'm not going to stand by and watch her——"

"For God's sake, Matthew! We're better parents than most, and of course you're standing by and watching her. That's all you've been doing for months. Watching and yelling."

"Now you're blaming me," he said.

"No, I'm not! You're blaming yourself. You think she inherited the tendency from you and that means you have to do something about it. Well, you can't do a damn thing. Nothing you've tried has worked." Matthew rubbed a hand over his eyes. His palms smelled of beer, and suddenly he felt ill. All those years of work, of study, of success; the beautiful home in the beautiful place, the family vacations, the piano lessons. Molly was right: he'd done everything he could think of to protect Katie, and it hadn't worked. It hadn't been good enough. He'd failed.

A breeze smelling of warm, wet earth blew in through the kitchen window, and he thought he heard a throaty chuckling noise outside. Silly, he told himself. There are no forests for miles, and it was just a dream. But suddenly his tongue tasted of garbage and rotting leaves, and he was cold despite the warmth of the day.

"Matt?" Molly said. "What's wrong?"

He couldn't look at her. He stared al his fingers, remembering the sharp pieces of butterfly slide on the schoolroom floor, the gleam of moonlight on pointed teeth. Could trying to protect people be evil? If he'd let the little people feast on his father, that winter night, would Katie have been safe?

"Matthew, your hands are shaking. What is it?"

He swallowed. "Did I ever tell you about that nightmare I had when I was a kid?" He knew he hadn't; he'd never told anyone. Why should he? He'd outgrown his mother's superstitions. It had only been a dream.

"No," Molly said. "Tell me now."

So he did, trying to laugh as he told her about his mother's stories, about Miss Summersong and Nutmeg and the freezing midwinter night when the little people had come to claim the evil in the house. "It was just a dream," he said when he was finished; and then, smelling her perfume across the table, "I think I fell in love with you because you reminded me of Miss Summersong."

"Thank you," she said gravely, and smiled. "I fell in love with you because you were the first man I'd ever met who admired bacteria and remembered the titles of all the Narnia books. Matthew, what if the little people were real?"

"If they were, it didn't do any good." The taste of garbage was gone; all he could smell now was honeysuckle. He got up and went to the window. The front yard stretched smooth and vibrant and empty to the road; a red sportscar sped by, too fast, filled with shouting teenagers. Katie, Matthew thought, his fear returning. "I drove them away with Miss Summersong's charm. I didn't let them have anything evil because I was afraid they'd hurt us. I was afraid my father wouldn't believe in them even when he saw them there, and that they'd kill him."

"I think you're wrong," she said. "I think they went away because you fed them."

"Then why didn't anything change? Why didn't the evil stop?"

"Because it wasn't evil at all, but illness and ignorance. Because the only evil you can give away is your own. Look— your grandfather gave up the behavior that was hurting him and his family, right? Well, maybe what you fed the little people that night was your *belief* that you were evil. Maybe that's what was hurting you most. Does that make sense?"

"No," he said, and heard chuckling again. He gripped the windowsill and peered outside, into the beginnings of dusk. No one was there. Go away, he thought. Go away and leave me alone. "If I gave it to them, why do I still have it?"

"Because it grew back," Molly said softly. "Like a fingernail, or a strand of hair." She came up behind him and held him for a long time, her arms around his waist and her face pressed against his shoulder. He allowed himself to be enveloped by the familiar smell of lavender, and finally he turned and kissed her.

"There's a meeting at the high school in half an hour," she said into the hollow of his breastbone. "For parents who are scared about drugs." She laughed, sounding embarrassed, and Matthew realized how hard she was working to keep her voice steady. "You know—what to look for, where to get help, that kind of thing. Do you want to come me with me?"

"No," he said. He couldn't face it in public, not yet. "Come back and tell me about it."

"All right." She pulled away from him and gathered up her purse und keys. "Try not to yell at Katie if she comes home."

He nodded numbly and went back to stand, unseeing, at the kitchen window. He wondered if he could still remember the titles of all the Narnia chronicles, and found that he could. I like myself because I like good books, he thought. I like myself because I'm a good scientist. I like myself because I've been as good a parent as I knew how to be, even if I wasn't enough, even if I made too many mistakes.

It occurred to him that maybe he had loved Katie too much, been too proud of her, jinxed her somehow. "Take whatever bad stuff you want," he said aloud, speaking quietly because he felt foolish. He wondered if the neighbors could hear him through the open window. "Take away as much garbage as you can carry, but leave me what I love. Give me back what I love and I'll never ask you for anything again."

All he could smell was honeysuckle. And what good would it do, even if they were real? What could they return to him? His parents were dead, and at last he realized, aching, that Molly was right: Katie belonged only to herself. She'd have to make her own offerings.

He was very tired. He closed his eyes, leaning against the windowsill, and breathed in the smell of flowers. A dog barked in the distance, and when Matthew opened his eyes again he saw Nutmeg, as spry as she'd been on the day she vanished, trotting across the tranquil twilit lawn with a squirrel in her mouth.

On a Phantom Tide

WILLIAM F. WU

Introduction

William F. Wu's Jack Hong series had a home at Pulphouse. *Jack Hong, who chases a* kei-lun, *a Chinese unicorn, across the American West, gives us a clear-eyed view of what life was like for Chinese immigrants in the 19ᵗʰ century.*

That history is one of Bill's specialties. His doctoral dissertation for the University of Michigan was published as a standalone volume called The Yellow Peril: ChineseAmericans in American Fiction, 1850-1940.

The Jack Hong series is one that would not have seen print without Pulphouse. *And, quite frankly, still needs to be read in light of all events of the past few years here in the States. You can find all of the Jack Hong stories in* A Temple of Forgotten Spirits: The Complete Stories of Jack Hong.

On a Phantom Tide

William F. Wu

I was standing on the rich Iowa turf by a highway in the middle of nowhere. All night, I had shivered in the back of a pickup truck in a thunderstorm, huddled in a heavy canvas tarp. Now, in the earliest hint of dawn, I was cold and dizzy with exhaustion.

The keilin had been here, though—the Chinese unicorn. I had only seen a flash of it, as always, but that was enough. With horses' hooves, a fleshy horn, and all different colors on its back, it was hard to mistake for anything else.

I started to walk.

The sky was clear now and I hiked, soaked and shivering, into a little town. It was the kind with a main drag on six blocks of highway and a four-way blinking red light in the center. I could hear rainwater running in the sewers. The residential area was big, though, and old. It seemed rich, in a 1930s sort of way.

The early sun was bright, and it seemed too hot for an early midwestern June this far north. At least it was drying me off.

The town was still asleep. Everything was still wet and a sparkling haze hung in the air. Squinting in the bright light, I looked over a Gulf station casually, like I wanted a restroom. It was a small, tight place with no service area, just gas pumps and the office. The restrooms and pop machines and all the empty bottles were inside. I used the side of the building for effect, in case anyone was watching.

I reached a Standard station a block farther up. Their wooden racks of empties were stacked outside by the back door. I picked up two full racks, all I could carry easily, and circled around to the front. It wasn't my best scam, but it was easy and pretty safe. I didn't feel up to much. Since I hadn't eaten for a while, the bottles were heavy. I sat down across the street on the porch of a bank where the steps were dry and yawned for a while.

Traffic picked up. A tall, skinny guy in white work clothes and a light blue baseball cap came to open the Standard station. I went over with the bottles and set them down on the floor in front of the pop machine with bottles. Another one had cans. The guy ran around opening doors and wheeling racks of new tires out of the bays into the driveway.

One bay had a huge motorcycle in it, the kind I occasionally saw ridden in packs on the highway. I watched him through a ring of white sparkles on the edges of my vision.

"Help ya," he said, switching his baseball cap for a Standard one. The name "Marc" was stitched in cursive on his shirt pocket in red thread. His brown hair looked slimy.

I waved at the bottles. "How much?"

He glanced down and frowned. "Register's empty, 'cept for the change I'll need. Sorry." He started back into the service area.

"I'll wait for some business."

He shrugged without stopping and went on in to clang things around.

I went out and sat on the step by the door where the sun was warm. Traffic was still light. I yawned twice. The rain had kept me from sleeping all night. I had gone about twenty hours without it, and none of them relaxing.

Marc came out and leaned on the doorframe. "It'll be a while, yet."

"Nothing but time." I slapped my face once, but it didn't help.

He looked down at me and put his hands in his pockets. "You're Chinese, ain'tcha?"

"Somebody was," I said. He didn't understand that, but he pretended to. I meant my ancestors, some four generations back, but I didn't feel like helping him with it.

"Where's your friend?"

At first I thought he meant the somebody. Then I wasn't sure. "You got me," I said, which was certainly true.

He went back inside to bang around some more.

A couple of cars rolled in for gas. I started counting them. A sort of white haze in my eyes kept obscuring them unless I blinked it away. I figured if just a few customers paid cash, he'd pay me for the bottles to get rid of me. He kept getting credit cards, though.

Chasing the keilin was a ridiculous occupation. I had seen it one night and just run off after it. I told other people I was just a drifter, but I was sure the keilin was leading me somewhere. Every so often, I glimpsed it waiting. When I changed direction to follow it, it vanished again.

The other Chinese guy came along about a minute later.

———

He was about five feet five, thin, with braces and heavy glasses. I guessed he was sixteen. He had a nervous, shy look. Only he wasn't Chinese, really; he was as American as I was.

He stopped dead when he saw me and looked around a little too anxiously, with a jerky smile.

"He's in there," I said, yanking a thumb toward the bays.

The new guy looked in but stayed where he was, fidgeting.

I stood up, feeling fidgety now myself. He looked up at me expectantly.

"I'm Jack Hong," I said, holding out my hand.

He lifted a limp hand, grinning. "Helmut Han," he said.

I suppressed a wince. Another Mandarin surname after a stupid first name. Or at least, I didn't like it. I could see the type. He looked like a doormat on legs, and would be a bookworm and a class-A wimp. Mandarin background, I guessed, and first generation.

"Hi," I said, letting go of his paw. He had a puppy's eyes and did everything else but wag his tail. I imitated the station guy's Iowa accent, saying, "You're Chinese, ain'tcha?"

He didn't get it, of course, having just come in. I didn't care.

"Yeah," he said, with a kind of goofy grin.

I looked into the service area. Marc was polishing the chrome on the chopper with a towel and flicking off lint with a snap. He'd left it in the bay all night; it didn't need any polishing.

"Go get him," I said. "He doesn't know you're here."

Helmut shrugged and blinked a couple of times slowly, squinting behind his glasses. "I'll just wait."

I went and banged on the glass door to the service area and then opened it. "Got a guy here."

Marc came in and looked down at Helmut with distaste. "Yeah?"

"Uh, I can't get the money here. There's no place to wire it to. But I can't take my car back on the highway, either."

Marc ran his fingers through his greasy hair and adjusted his cap. "Hell." He shrugged and started back.

"What is it?" I asked, loud enough to stop Marc. I looked at Helmut. "You got a car?"

"Yeah, a brown Pinto with a broken thermostat. It overheats every—"

I looked at Marc. "You can't fix it, eh?"

Marc looked annoyed. "'Course I can fix it. I can fix

anything I got parts for, and I got parts for that. He can't pay for it. Not my—"

"Lemme see." I held my hand out to Helmut.

"What?"

"Your wallet."

He chuckled nervously and handed it to me. I flipped through the contents fast, while Helmut watched carefully. Of course, he was too polite to show real disgust. He had one ten-dollar traveler's check, bank cards, and a bunch of gasoline credit cards, but none Standard took. "There," I said, tapping a Gulf card. "Use that."

"Not here." Marc sneered and started away.

I put a hand on the door handle in front of him. "Rig it with the place up the street. Any classy place can." I gave the card to him and returned Helmut's wallet.

Marc looked at me hard with an unfriendly half-smile. Then he looked up and moved his cap with one hand. I expected something to crawl out of the crud in his hair.

"What do you mean, bud?"

"Take it up the street and let 'em look over the card. They'll guarantee you payment when his money comes in through the Gulf card."

"Yeah?" Marc looked at the card as though it said something important. He couldn't think of an objection. "Hell." He stomped to the phone and dialed.

I glanced at Helmut, who was grinning at me happily. He was starting to scare me. I shushed him, even though he wasn't saying anything.

"Okay," said Marc, hanging up. "I read 'em the number and they okayed it. I didn't know places did that." He looked angry, though. "I just work here," he muttered.

Helmut's brown Pinto was parked in the station driveway where he'd brought it the night before. He drove it into one of the bays and got out. We waited while Marc pumped gas to a customer.

"How'd you get here?" I asked Helmut.

"Huh? Oh, I had to pull off yesterday when it overheated. I came real slowly along these little highways before I found a town. Then I had to stay in this old little motel, you know, the sign said 'Auto Court.' It was a real dump." He laughed a little.

"I spent the night in the back of a moving pickup truck," I said, grinning. "Trade you, next time."

Marc came back, looking mean. "I can start on it, but I have to pump gas, too. Can't work on it steady till another guy comes in, about ten. Understand?" He was hoping we'd get discouraged.

"Well, sure," said Helmut. "That's fine." He looked at me. "Have you eaten? I'll buy you breakfast." He made a face. "When I'm hungry, I eat. I hate to wait."

"Sure," I said, figuring that a high school kid with a car and credit cards could afford me. "There's a roadside place down there a mile or so." I inclined my head in the direction I had hiked in from.

"A mile?" Helmut blinked slowly. "I don't want to walk that far—"

"We don't have to walk at this hour. C'mon." I led him out to the side of the road.

Helmut chuckled nervously as I glanced up the road for cars.

"Sit down," I said, yawning.

"Huh?"

"Might as well sit. If it takes a while, you can stand and I'll sit." A car appeared over a little rise up the street and I stuck my right arm out straight, thumb up. The car went by.

"Ding hao," said Helmut, grinning.

"What?"

"Ding hao. It means, like, 'real good' in Mandarin. 'Just right.' You never heard that?"

"Nope."

"In World War II, they used to say it in China. With Americans. It meant 'thumbs up,' like that."

I looked at my thumb and finally got it. "Oh. Ding hao."

Helmut smiled, looking pleased that he had taught me something.

I watched him for a moment. "You, uh…know there was a legend about a Chinese unicorn?"

"Really?" He laughed. "No…I'm interested in real stuff."

He was normal—not like me. I yawned. I'd be better off making conversation. "You know this World War II stuff? Your family come here in '49, then?"

"Well, to Taiwan, first. Then here. But I studied it in college, too."

College?

A roar of machinery down the street caused me to turn. It was a big guy in brown leather and a red helmet coming fast on a huge bike whose noise drowned out everything else. He swung suddenly into the station, forcing Helmut and me to dive clear.

I rolled over on the grass and squinted after the guy. Some friend of Marc's, apparently. My head was spinning. Now that I was horizontal, I wanted to stay that way and go to sleep. But I really needed food.

Helmut grinned. "Guess he didn't see us."

I got up very slowly. "Sure he did. He just thought he'd have some fun." Helmut knew that. I looked toward the station. Marc was pointing toward us and laughing with his friend.

College, Helmut had said.

"How old are you?" I dusted myself off.

"Twenty-two."

"I'm twenty-four," I said, for something to say. I looked at him again. He could be twenty-two, all right; I'd just made the same mistake that others made about me all the time. And his braces threw me.

I looked back at Marc, talking and shrugging and gesturing at us. His friend took off his helmet and looked, too. I got it, then; as soon as the other employee came to work, Marc had planned to sneak off with his biker buddy, but now he had Helmut's car to fix.

"Put your thumb out," I said, over my shoulder, as I started back to the station.

They didn't see me coming. Both had turned and gone into the bays. When I got there, they were squatting down by the engine and poking at it and grinning. I went into the service area through the station room.

For a moment I stood just inside, watching them play around across the way. The new guy had carefully hung his jacket and helmet on a wall hook meant for tools. He was wearing a ragged turquoise T-shirt and I could see elaborate dark blue tattoos on his powerful arms. His hair was long, straggly, and blond under the filth. He had a short, full brown beard. Altogether he looked like a good guy and a fine drinkin' buddy to his friends. I didn't suppose I qualified.

Since they didn't seem to have noticed me, I wandered over and they both looked up over their shoulders.

"Yeah?" The new guy sneered.

"C'mon, Lee," said Marc, but he was laughing.

"Just thought I'd ask about the car," I said as firmly as I dared.

"I'll get to it," growled Marc. He sounded tougher, now that his friend was watching. "Finish it, maybe after lunch."

"Yeah, sure," I said.

Lee stood up, a gigantic hairy hulk that stunk with old sweat and leather. His face was shiny and he wiped it on his short sleeve. I backed up a little.

"'Yeah, sure,'" Lee whined, mimicking me. He laughed. "Get lost." He started making nasal noises he thought sounded like Chinese.

My judgement was lacking from no sleep. "So long, fatso," I said, turning.

A hard fist hit me in the back of the head so hard that I stumbled forward. Before I fell, a boot kicked me in the rear hard enough to straighten me up. I managed to keep my balance, and skipped out of the station to the hooting laughter behind me. They didn't follow me; I was lucky they were in a good mood.

When I stumbled out of the station, Helmut had a car stopped on the street with a teenaged guy at the wheel. I was amazed, but found the energy to run, clumsily, to catch them. The green grass ahead of me swam lazily in my vision, but I stayed upright and jumped into the front seat next to Helmut. He grinned proudly at getting us a ride.

The little roadside place had just a few customers. We slid into a booth with tan vinyl seats repaired with wide, ragged red plastic tape. Helmut flipped through the selections on the little silver jukebox, but my eyes stung when I tried to read the song titles. The waitress was a smiling high school girl with long brown hair, wearing a tight white plastic uniform. I drooled over the menu.

"Orange juice," I said, picking at random. "Hot tea. Ice water. Vegetable soup. The number two breakfast, eggs over easy. Cinnamon toast. Tomato juice, too. Reuben sandwich. How 'bout a Coke? Tossed salad with Italian dressing. Uh...."

Helmut looked up at the waitress, grinning. "I'll have the same." He caught my eye and we both started laughing.

"Okay...." She sang amiably, giggling as she walked away.

"I'm thirsty," I explained, feeling silly.

"That's okay. Hey, listen. Did you know...." Helmut earnestly launched into a whirl of historical facts about Chinese immigrants over a century ago. I guessed he'd learned it in college. Teaching me made him feel good. I was too tired to concentrate and let most of it go by until he got to white ship captains sneaking illegal Chinese immigrants into San Francisco on their ships.

"Yeah, man," he said, just as the food began arriving. "They were packed in like on slave ships, and all of 'em chained together."

"What?"

"Chained together, so they couldn't get away and cause trouble on board to get better treatment." He grinned. "Listen, if the ship captains were about to be caught by the authorities, they'd just chuck 'em all overboard, chains and all—let 'em sink." He chuckled nervously and looked in surprise at the amount of food placed in front of him. "They were treated just like inanimate cargo, or animals."

"Huh." I started eating, with visions of starving and chained Chinamen drowning in my soup. Helmut went on talking while we ate, but the white haze around my head seemed to fog out everything except my food and the splashing of chains and flailing bodies in my mind.

When I finally finished, my stuffed stomach hurt with the unaccustomed intake. I leaned back in the booth and looked up. Helmut was talking about Chinese junks in San Francisco Bay.

"Jack London wrote about 'em there. So did other people. They used to catch shrimp and carry cargo and all kinds of stuff. Only you never hear about them now. It's like they never existed, even though they did."

"What happened to them?" I felt guilty for not listening while I had been eating. Helmut had more substance than I had thought.

He shrugged. "Sank, I guess." He laughed. "Sank, burned, I don't know."

I nodded. "Interesting. I never knew this stuff."

"Really?" He looked pleased. "Hey, when the car's fixed, I'll take you around. You wanna?"

"Sure." I grinned. "We can watch all the Asian women with white guys." I laughed looking away and he laughed and then I caught his eye and we both laughed. I laughed a lot. I laughed at him for appreciating it and I laughed at myself for knowing what would make him laugh. Then I laughed at myself for laughing. The only thing I didn't laugh at was all the Asian women with white guys.

I was starting to like the slob.

"How come you helped me?"

"Huh?" I hesitated, surprised.

"I really appreciate it."

"Oh…yeah, sure." I avoided looking at him. I wasn't sure why I had helped, except that he hadn't seemed capable of helping himself. More important, though, was the keilin. It had come this way, led me here. Its appearance was auspicious; good events occurred where it went.

Helmut paid the check and I staggered outside, so drowsy I could hardly walk. I could hear Helmut following me, but I was too weary to consider him. We went out onto the grass near the highway and I crumpled to the earth. "I gotta sleep," I muttered, by way of apology.

Falling asleep on him just gave me more to feel guilty about, but I had no choice. Besides, I was too tired to feel guilt, or anything else. My body was finally taking control, after I had abused it through sheer will. Anyway, Helmut's car wouldn't be ready for hours.

The grass was cool and green, the ground hard and flat. Yet I sank into it all, descending from sunlight, from traffic, from bugs. Helmut and my tight belt and boots and all the hassles of the road stayed somewhere on the surface of my mind, left far behind. I flowed downward, falling slowly through a sea of green shapes and blue shadows. Choking, water-logged, bug-eyed yellow faces came whirling lazily down past me in brightly-lit water, limbs kicking and stroking in a frantic slow-motion dance. Their trailing black queues swirled and flipped like sleepy kite-tails and the chains shackling their ankles and wrists clanked dully in the water, pulling the prisoners steadily downward. They left me behind and darkness fell over a dreamless sleep.

The heat woke me up. My clothes were soaked in sweat and

I was groggy from sleeping in the muggy June afternoon. Even so, I had slept for hours, judging by the sun.

I rolled over, wiped my face on my sleeve, and looked around. The sun was bright. A car went by.

Helmut was gone. Taking a deep breath, I pushed myself erect and started back to the little restaurant. Standing up in the breeze was cool. The sleep helped a lot, but not enough. One afternoon in the heat was not very restful.

Still waking up, I walked a crooked line to the door and went inside to collapse on a booth. Helmut wasn't there, either. Now that I was in the air conditioning, my mind began to clear.

The same waitress came up. "Your friend left a message. I promised to tell you he's gone back to the station?" She turned it into a question at the end, like she wasn't sure she had it right.

"Okay. Could I have some ice water?"

"Sure."

While I sat staring still glassy-eyed at the far wall, another question occurred to me. I was yawning when she came back with the water, but I motioned for her to wait till I finished. "I was, uh, wondering if you know how he went back into town. Did he walk?"

"Oh, no. I saw him out the window. He hitchhiked."

"Thanks." I finished the water quickly and asked for more. Altogether, I drank four glasses fast and another one slowly. I was vaguely pleased that Helmut had had the guts to thumb alone. Nothing would happen to him at this short distance in midday.

Chuckling at this new protective concern, I went out to the little highway and stood waiting. After ten minutes and only four cars, I started walking. By the time I finally got a ride, I had already covered all but a hundred yards of the trip, but every little ride helps. I found Helmut sitting on the same bank porch where I had sat across the street from the station.

Helmut grinned as I came up the steps. The sunlight flashed on his braces. "Did you have a nice nap?"

"I guess." I sat down. I hadn't thought of collapsing exhausted on the earth and lying uncovered outside as a nap, exactly. "Say, aren't they done yet?"

Helmut shrugged, blinking nervously at the station across the street. His bravery was coming one step at a time. "The truck came in a while ago."

Not much of an answer. I sighed. "Okay."

I got up and started across the street. By this time, I was fully awake and feeling my lunch and my sleep. I could hear Helmut following me.

A semi with a gray trailer and green lettering was angled across the doors to the bays. The empty cab was up and steam issued from its insides. Only an emergency would bring a big rig into a little station like this. Marc walked around in circles in the bays, nodding, while the trucker followed him, jabbering into his ear.

Helmut's Pinto was in one of the bays with the hood down. Lee was leaning against it, monkeying around in a tool chest. I waited outside, watching as Marc picked up a length of rope and started coiling it. The trucker was getting more excited. Finally Marc followed him out to the truck and started tinkering around. The new guy was pumping gas to a customer and wiping the windshield. We'd have to wait for Marc, on account of the weird credit arrangement.

I didn't want to interrupt an angry trucker and confronting Lee would be worse. Folding my arms, I leaned against the back of the semi. Helmut joined me. I wasn't any braver than he was, at the moment.

"I think it's done," I said. Marc had had plenty of time. The clock in the station said it was six-thirty p.m.

"That'd be nice." Helmut went to stand behind Marc and his greasy hair.

I stood there doing nothing, just looking around, and heard Marc say that the truck just had a broken hose clamp that he could fix right away. When he started back for the station,

Helmut caught up with him. Marc nodded as they entered and I relaxed a little. I also figured out why nothing disgusting had crawled out of Marc's hair. Even vermin died in it.

Marc had dropped his coil of rope over a rack of new tires. One end hung from the rack, swinging very slightly. It was quarter-inch orange plastic rope and it started me thinking.

Helmut came up grinning. "All set. Wanna go?"

I looked into the service area where Lee was walking around and messing with his bike. "Go on up the hill about a block," I told him. "Keep the engine running and my door open."

He blinked at me uncertainly.

"Just go on," I said, smiling confidently. It reassured him.

I waited a long time. First I waited for Lee to leave the bays, which he finally did to join Marc in working on the truck. I took the coil of rope and started looping the ends. My timing would have to be just right.

When Marc had finished with the truck, the cab went down and the driver walked into the station with Marc and Lee. I tensed, waiting to see if Lee would kill the scheme by returning to his bike. He didn't, so I scooted in through an open bay door and looped one end of the rope over the big handlebars of Lee's bike—not Marc's. I ducked out quickly and wound the other end of the rope around one of the big door handles at the back of the truck. Everything depended on them, which was a lousy way to plan anything.

A few more minutes passed and I knew Helmut would be worrying and wanting to come back. I was sure he wouldn't, though, since I'd told him to wait. He could do me a real favor this time, instead of lecturing at me.

The trucker mounted his cab and fired up. Lee and Marc started into the service area but didn't notice the rope right away. They did when the truck started forward, though, and the rope tightened.

I hopped onto the ledge at the back of the moving truck and watched as the motorcycle was pulled over on its side and dragged out the open door of the bay, screeching and tearing on the concrete. Lee ran out screaming while Marc skipped alongside the bike, trying to grab the rope off the handlebars. It was too taut.

I caught Lee's eye and blew him a kiss. He ran after the truck, yelling every insult at his command—about two. Pounding his fists against the air over his head, he screamed, red-faced and horrible, still chasing me as the truck picked up speed.

Suddenly the driver slowed, looking back out of the cab window to see what the noise was about. I jumped off and ran for my life.

I didn't look back for Lee, but a guy like him can worship his machine and Lee seemed ready to kill for it. Breathing hard, I charged up the hill toward the open door of the Pinto wondering if I'd miscalculated my energy. The rear of the Pinto bounced and blurred in my eyes as I ran and the foggy white faces appeared on either side of me, staring as I ran a corridor between them. But this time they were laughing, too, and they all wore long, transparent queues flying behind them. Then I heard Lee's footsteps and struggling breath closing in.

The Pinto suddenly lurched forward away from me, swung into a tight U-turn toward us with a squeal of tires, and came down the hill. This kid was okay, after all. Helmut slammed on the brakes and I leaped into the car with Lee's hands clawing and tugging at my shirt. He couldn't get a grip, though, and Helmut launched the car with a roar and a jerk that swung the door shut behind me. I slammed back against the seat, laughing.

———

For a while I watched out the rear window to see if Lee would appear behind us on Marc's bike, but he didn't. Finally I settled into my seat and told Helmut about it. He laughed nervously but his grin had that same puppy-eyed awe that made me feel strange.

"You know where we're goin'?" I asked him, to change the subject.

"Oh, yeah. The guy at the station told me how to get to I-35. It'll take a while, but it's real simple. We just—"

"Which guy? The one there this morning?"

"Uh, yeah."

"Mm." I didn't like having Marc know our short-term destination. "Well, just keep driving," I said. "We have a good lead."

"Good."

I gazed out the window without seeing anything. I had not seen the keilin since just before dawn, and was afraid that I was losing its trail. Still, it would reveal itself again when it wished, I was sure. Cars and bikers and highways seemed like an odd world for a Chinese unicorn, but I believed in it—I had seen it, more than once.

I decided I could do nothing at the moment. Gradually, the rhythm of the car began lulling me to sleep. I curled up in my seat and closed my eyes.

"You ever hit anybody?"

"What?" I opened my eyes and sat up.

Helmut laughed. "People walk all over me. I've, well, never done anything that took any guts. You're really a, you know, a hero type."

I grimaced. "What I did was pretty stupid. That guy wants to kill both of us, I'm sure. Staying alive is more important. Really."

"*You* can say that." Helmut looked over at me and dropped the nervous laughter. "I wish I'd done what you did. In fact, I wish I'd done practically anything. I've never even stood up for myself, let alone anyone else. You just stepped right in."

"Glad to help," I said lamely. I curled up in my seat again and closed my eyes. Soon I was asleep again.

I woke up in darkness, alone. The car was stopped and felt

cold, like it had been parked for a while. I sat up and rubbed my face with the heel of one hand. Forcing myself to wake up quickly was becoming tiresome. So to speak. Well, since it was dark, we were well away from that particular little town and its gas station.

I opened the car door slowly and climbed out. A little roadside restaurant faced me. The light from it cast a dim glow over the nearly deserted parking lot. Helmut was just having dinner without me.

The air was pleasantly cool. I walked around a little to get the blood moving and then stopped suddenly. We weren't on any interstate. A little highway ran past the restaurant, the same one we had taken out of that little town, according to the sign near the streetlight. What had Helmut said before breakfast? When he's hungry, he eats.

Trying to sort it out, I realized that if we'd been stopped for long, Helmut would be finished soon. Instead of rushing in to haul him out, I decided to stay where I was and watch for Lee— or rather, listen for a chopper in the distance. I stayed well away from the Pinto, in the shadows by the highway.

Nothing happened, but I stayed alert, adrenalin flowing. Lee had loved his bike too much not to try catching us, and he could have borrowed Marc's. I had been too careless of Helmut's innocence when I assumed that he would know better than to stop before the interstate, where we could lose ourselves. I wondered if those weird pale faces were watching—and what they were.

Then, just up the highway, I saw it—not the big motorcycle, but a pale equine shape standing in profile, switching its tail. The horn on its head stood out clearly for just a moment. Then it turned and cantered soundlessly up the highway, to disappear in the darkness.

A flash of light behind me made me jump. The restaurant door had opened. It was Helmut, but he hadn't seen me right away. I started toward him and then the roar of a huge motorcycle thundered from the darkness along one side of the restaurant. Lee had just been waiting to get us both on foot at once.

"Get in the car!" I screamed, but Helmut turned from it and ran toward me as Lee circled around the few other cars in the lot. "C'mon! C'mon!" I waved frantically, running away toward the highway myself. Lee seemed to be alone, probably because he had hurried.

Lee's shadow had one heavy booted leg cocked to get us as he passed. As Lee's great dark metal monster closed in, I tackled Helmut and threw us both onto the shoulder of the road. We were on the grass now, away from the lights of the little restaurant. I leaped up, dragging Helmut back toward the faint light of the parking lot. Lee circled and cut us off, so we had to run back again.

This time, as we ran, he singled me out. Light from his bike caught me like a stage spot and stayed on me, no matter how I dodged, as he roared toward me. I hurdled the roadside ditch, fell, and turned wide-eyed to watch him come.

As the big white headlight grew gigantic, Helmut flung himself at me in probably the only tackle he had ever tried. He was blindsided by the chopper and never touched me. The collision was horrible, a thump and a shriek of metal against the asphalt of the road as the cycle skidded and Lee fell spinning to one side. I half-crawled, half-ran into a clump of bushes and trees.

Helmut was dead when the cycle hit him and dead again when he slammed neck-snapping into a tree. Lee got up painfully, forcing the bike into control again with sheer muscle. He swept the trees and bushes with his headlight, knowing he'd left a witness. I was out of sight, though, acting dead.

Lee yelled something at me, but the rumble of his machine drowned it out. Then he turned and sped down the highway into the night. I stood and watched his headlight shrink in the distance.

Helmut had found his courage at the wrong moment—for

himself. I had never owed my life to anyone before, especially for his single reckless, gutsy move. This time someone had actually done something for me—something important. I felt tears coming, but not only from sorrow.

I turned away into the darkness of the trees, taking deep breaths. Trees in Iowa, I thought idiotically. I thought this was prairie country.

The appearance of the keilin was auspicious. My meeting up with Helmut would have been good—if not for the choice he had just made. Or perhaps the keilin knew better than I.

I heard wood creaking loudly above me. Still stunned, I looked up, smelling the sharp salt breeze of an ocean. A huge white ship, splintered and blasted, hovered over us in the night blackness—a Chinese junk with its mast broken and the top section hanging bent toward me, tatters of sail trailing in the wind. Bits of board hung from holes ripped out of the hull and frayed rope swung from the swaying top section of mast and over the sides of the junk. The hull was crusted with barnacles and smeared with the slime of the deep, gathered before this phantom was raised to the star-splashed sky.

The ship wasn't the worst of it.

Faces crowded the railing of the hull. Figures hung from the broken mast and the torn rigging. Wraiths in rags, skeletons in rotted clothing, grinning skulls yet with long, braided queues all packed the pale and wispy craft. Every one of them was chained together.

As I watched, they threw something down—a glowing, translucent chain that clanked as it sailed through the air. The end of it touched down at the lifeless body on the ground and when the silent figures on the junk began to pull up the chain, a limp human form dangled and swayed from the end of it.

As fleshless fingers hoisted the sagging shape aboard, one white face turned and looked at me, dark eye sockets locking to mine. His queue waved in the wind. A great-great grandfather, maybe. Or a great-great-great uncle. He knew me and I got it.

He knew everything I had ever been, everything I had ever done. He knew my dusty roads and my lonely soul.

He knew the keilin, that had led me here.

The empty black eyes held my gaze as the junk drifted away on a phantom tide, fading and floating into the darkness of the sky, the one face still staring. I watched until it was gone.

If there was a body lying near me, I didn't want to see it, because what if it wasn't there.

I started to move, but my wrists were locked—only for a moment. I felt the cold damp press of century-old irons binding my hands together, stinking of rotting seaweed. Then it was gone.

Slowly, I brought my eyes down all the way to my feet. I was standing on the rich Iowa turf in the middle of nowhere. The air was cool. A car hummed faintly in the distance. I stepped out of the trees and went slowly to the edge of the highway. When the headlights hit me, I extended my arm and stuck up my thumb. *Ding hao.*

Acknowledgments

This book would not exist without help from:

Bill Trojan, Philip Barnhart, Nina Kiriki Hoffman, Jon Gustafson, Mark Budz, Lynn Adams, Alan Bard Newcomer, Kevin Kenan, Stephanie Haddock, Jerry Oltion, Adrian Nikolas Phoenix, Jonathon Bond, Greg Freeman, Becky Connor, Todd Vandemark, Kevin J. Anderson, Charles N. Brown, Richard Curtis, Gordon Van Gelder, Kij Johnson, Harlan Ellison, Charles de Lint, Edward Bryant, Jack Williamson, Steve Rasnic Tem, William F. Wu, and all the book dealers, subscribers, writers, and readers who have believed in us from the beginning.

About the Editor

KRISTINE KATHRYN RUSCH

New York Times bestselling author Kristine Kathryn Rusch writes in almost every genre. Generally, she uses her real name (Rusch) for most of her writing. Under that name, she publishes best-selling science fiction and fantasy, award-winning mysteries, acclaimed mainstream fiction, controversial nonfiction, and the occasional romance. Her novels have made bestseller lists around the world and her short fiction has appeared in eighteen best of the year collections. She has won more than twenty-five awards for her fiction, including the Hugo, *Le Prix Imaginales*, the *Asimov's* Readers Choice award, and the *Ellery Queen Mystery Magazine* Readers Choice Award.

Publications from *The Chicago Tribune* to *Booklist* have included her Kris Nelscott mystery novels in their top-ten-best mystery novels of the year. The Nelscott books have received nominations for almost every award in the mystery field, including the best novel Edgar Award, and the Shamus Award.

She writes goofy romance novels as award-winner Kristine Grayson.

She also edits. Beginning with work at the innovative publishing company, Pulphouse, followed by her award-winning tenure at *The Magazine of Fantasy & Science Fiction*, she took fifteen years off before returning to editing with the original anthology series *Fiction River*, published by WMG Publishing. She acts as series editor with her husband, writer Dean Wesley Smith.

To keep up with everything she does, go to kriswrites.com and sign up for her newsletter. To track her many pen names and series, see their individual websites (krisnelscott.com, kristinegrayson.com, retrievalartist.com, divingintothewreck.com, fictionriver.com, pulphousemagazine.com).